The Girl In His Dreams

Terri Ely

ISBN-13: 9781534600737
ISBN-10: 1534600736

This book is dedicated to
my mother,
a truly amazing woman.

Contents

Acknowledgements

I thank God for the inspiration and the words for this story.

I am also grateful to Phyllis Hobe, a Guideposts editor and friend, who insisted that *The Girl in His Dreams* was not just a story but a book.

So many people have supported me these last ten years as I wrote and rewrote this book. Foremost among them are my patient husband, Gene, and my sons: Jerry and his wife, Julie; Patrick and his wife, Krista; Ken and his wife, Sandy; and Tom.

As a teenager, my grandson Ryan made an important observation about the story as it was written at that time. It caused me to change the direction of the book, and I thank him for that.

Extended family who supplied me with background and publishing information: Stephen E. Markert Sr., Candy Walsh, Carrie Dager, Sue Cea, Jeff and Margaret Pullman, Laura DiPietro, and Robert Littleton.

Friends who encouraged me in so many ways on my journey include Judy Oliver, my best friend who has encouraged me to write stories since we were in grade school; Alice Corey, who sent me notes and called me every now and then to ask, "How's the book coming?"; Irene Ganter, who helped with early research; and others such as Maxine Lewis, Dot Connor, Ann Marie Fantini, Bob Carman, Betty Ann Foster, and Gail Robinson, who listened to my book dilemmas and did kind favors for me.

Authors who guided me along the way include my faithful writing partner, Sharron Morita; Catherine Frompovich; Judy Brett; and Mary Ann Vincent, another CreateSpace author.

Editor Mary Murray volunteered her assistance and put me on the right track in telling my story.

Special people who transcribed the antiquated Palmer Shorthand in many of the letters that appear in the book include Jim Gillogly, a world-famous cryptographer who transcribed the first few passages, and Reba Lummis, a retired secretary, who began to transcribe passages in the rest of the letters at age 99, completing the last one at age 103!

Without question the biggest thank-you goes to my sister, Marge DiPietro, a cheerleader from day one and an excellent editor. With her suggestions and advice throughout the numerous revisions these past few years, I was finally able to finish *The Girl in His Dreams*.

Dear Reader,

This novel is based on a real story—one that occurred in my own family. In the very beginning, when I was laying the foundation for the story, I sent an e-mail one night to my four sons, appealing for their memories of this time in their grandmother's life. The next morning, I received the following from my oldest son, Jerry:

I remember Grandmom and me sitting on the couch in the living room one day. It was sometime after her mysterious Romeo had been found out but was still quite a new development. We were talking, and I must have asked her about him. How could I resist? She would light up whenever he was mentioned. She started out talking about a recent call or some event he was cooking up to visit her, but before I knew it, Grandmom was going on about how crazy it all seemed. How crazy it was for two people "their age" carrying on like a couple of teenagers. And in the briefest moment, she had the glow of a young girl talking about some boy of recent interest.

We had several of these conversations over time, and I always enjoyed them. It was wonderful to think of Grandmom dating! I thought it was great for both of them. It kept them vital just to stay in contact with each other. She had something new to think about. She liked that he wanted to do things and not act old, and she absolutely became younger for a while. Usually, at least early on, she would say that it was like a fairy tale, and sometimes she would blush and ask, "Don't you think this is ridiculous?" She seemed to be looking for a bit of validation for what to do with these feelings that she obviously felt did not belong in such an old body.

I always told her that I thought it was wonderful for her to feel this way and for her to enjoy it thoroughly. It seemed like this was sent from heaven—a reward for all her years of caring for her family.

But for sure, her Romeo's story is positively the stuff of fairy tales.

Prologue

The door of the small-town post office opened for the day precisely at eight, admitting a man of medium height wearing a dark overcoat and a gray tweed cap. Withdrawing a large white envelope from his inside coat pocket, he went directly to a middle-aged female clerk behind the counter. "Good morning, Janet," he said as he shoved the envelope and the exact change toward her. "Would you handstamp this, please?"

"We don't usually handstamp regular mail, Mr. Benson."

"Could you make an exception this time? It's important."

Eyeing him curiously, she replied, "Well, I guess I can for you."

A moment later she brought a small metal machine down hard on his envelope, leaving a round imprint showing the date and a ten-digit number indicating the post office's location but not the name of the town.

"That will get there for sure by tomorrow, won't it?" he asked.

"Absolutely. We have a mail truck leaving in an hour. Sending something special?"

The man's face relaxed into a smile, and his blue eyes sparkled. He winked and said, "Oh yes. Very special."

Part 1
The Mystery

Chapter 1

Rosemarie had not an inkling of the impending romantic intrigue that was about to disrupt her well-ordered life when she left home that snowy December morning. The small widow, bundled in black wool slacks, pink and black tweed jacket, wide-brimmed black felt hat, and black leather boots, strode briskly, as she did every day, along her one-mile route to Saint Mary's Church. Bound for eight o'clock Mass, she was heedless of the icy flakes pelting her face. Her thoughts were centered on her birthday lunch with her daughters. She reached church early, walked up the center aisle, and took her place in the second pew up front, on the right.

Two pews behind her, Caroline Hutchins, a stout, gray-haired, fiftyish woman, wished she had worn something other than her stained brown trench coat and tattered gray boots. She watched with admiration as Rosemarie opened the flap on her black leather shoulder bag and deposited a pair of stylish leather gloves. *Rosemarie always dresses like a lady*, she thought, *even on a snowy day like today.*

Oblivious of Caroline's appraisal, Rosemarie focused on the cross behind the main altar and prayed silently, "Thank you, God, for another birthday, good health, and my wonderful family. You have blessed me with so much, but sometimes I wonder what will happen to me when I can no longer take care of my home or myself. So many of my friends are moving in with their children or moving into apartments. I really don't want to do that, but I can't help worrying about the future."

Rosemarie would never admit to anyone but God that she was worried. By her demeanor and dress, she always gave the impression that she was confident and self-assured. However, that was far from the truth when Mike died suddenly four years before. At that time her friends and family were amazed how quickly she seemed to adjust to life on her own after more than sixty years of marriage. Little did they know that she didn't have a clue about paying bills or maintaining a house. Mike, an accountant, was the master of their castle. He handled those things all their married life. That was his job in their home. Hers was to cook, clean the house, and raise their two girls. Their system worked perfectly until…

We should have talked about what we would do when one of us died, Rosemarie thought ruefully after the funeral, when all of the company had gone. Her oldest daughter, Anne, helped her deal with the funeral expenses and unusual paperwork that came after Mike's death, but Rosemarie was loath to admit her ignorance about everyday bills and the house's maintenance. She muddled along in the beginning, not saying anything to anyone about differences in the checkbook or late notices on bills, but eventually, she realized that if she was going to remain independent, she had to do better. She began to keep all the bills in a box in the kitchen. She studied the bankbook closely to see when Mike wrote the monthly checks and followed his example. In a few months, she had the hang of it.

The house repairs were another troubling issue. She panicked the first time she discovered a leaky pipe in the basement. What was the plumber's name? Where did Mike keep those telephone numbers? She searched in his bureau, his desk, and boxes of old bills. Finally, she remembered the bulletin board on the landing in the basement. There she found neat rows of business cards and soiled scraps of paper thumbtacked to the board, with phone numbers for anyone who had ever done work for them—Harvey's Plumbing was among them.

"Dear God," she prayed, "You helped me then, please help me to trust in you now."

Suddenly, the silence in the semi darkened church was broken by the tinkling of brass bells indicating the beginning of Mass. Rosemarie left her worries with God and reached for the prayer book on the seat behind her, unaware that at that moment, a mail truck was wending its way through town with a mysterious letter that would ultimately enter her home and change her life.

Chapter 2

An hour later, her face rosy from the cold, Rosemarie bent to retrieve the newspaper from the top step of her white clapboard home. She laughed as a stream of white flakes cascaded to the step from the brim of her hat. Snow made her happy. It covered up the ugliness of winter and made everything beautiful.

She stood for a moment, paper in hand, savoring the scene. Looking up at the two-story colonial home she never dreamed she would have, she smiled with satisfaction. Then, glancing through the whitened tree limbs down the snow-covered street, she recalled how fate had brought her to this place.

When she and Mike married, they never imagined living anyplace but Philadelphia, where they were both born and raised. But after their daughters were born, they began to see things differently. The row houses on busy streets where they lived and the cement alleyways where they played when they were growing up somehow felt all wrong for their children. They wanted their precious little girls to run and tumble in green grass instead of skinning their hands and knees on cement as they did. Rosemarie smiled as she remembered how shocked their friends and family were when they did the unthinkable and moved to a small town in New Jersey. Their first home on a street lined with maple trees was an old, peeling, wooden house with a wobbly garage, but it had a yard with green grass. The girls thrived. She learned to garden, and Mike became an expert in home repair. They were happy.

As time passed, they had a new dream—a home in the colonial upscale town of Haddonfield, graced with picturesque parks, charming shops, and stately well-kept homes.

She remembered how long it took them to sell their old house. Years. Mike figured out how much they needed for a down payment on a house in Haddonfield, and that's what they asked for their home. He insisted that someday a young couple from Philadelphia would be looking for a place in the country for their family—just as they had done—and that couple would be willing to buy their place at his price. He was right. They made it to Haddonfield by the time their girls were in high school.

Suddenly feeling cold, Rosemarie stopped reminiscing, tucked the newspaper under her arm, pulled the keys from her handbag, and opened the front door. Time to get busy. Hanging her coat and hand-bag in the hall closet, she donned an apron and began her Thursday-morning routine of laundry and vacuuming. At ten o'clock she stopped for a cup of coffee and a bowl of Cheerios. Grabbing the newspaper from the counter, she eased into her seat at the kitchen table, eying Mike's empty chair across from her. Her heart ached—especially today.

He never forgot her birthday. If he were here, he would have a special gift for her. He always did.

Closing her eyes, she pictured one birthday she would never forget. It began in this room.

She was frying bacon on the stove that morning, feeling blue. Lost in thought, she didn't hear Mike come into the kitchen nor did she see him slip something under the table.

Sneaking up behind her, he whispered in her ear, teasing as always, "Happy birthday, kid. This is the big five-0, you know. Do you feel old yet?"

She jumped and scrunched up her face, replying grumpily, "You don't have to rub it in, do you? Let's just forget about it."

"No way!" Marching around the table, he belted out the "Happy Birthday" song at the top of his lungs. Then, stopping at her place, he deposited a card on her plate.

She had to laugh. Suddenly, her gloomy mood lifted. She felt like a kid at a birthday party. Her devilish Irishman, paunchy at fifty-two, with salt-and-pepper hair, could always make her laugh—even this day when she reached that dreaded age.

When breakfast was on the table, she pulled her chair out to sit.

The scene unfolded in her mind like it happened yesterday.

She screamed. There on her seat lay a wooden nutcracker doll with a tall black fur hat and bright-red uniform.

She hugged the doll to her and said between tears, "Mike, I've wanted a nutcracker ever since I was a kid. How did you know?"

Grinning from ear to ear, he said, "There's something else. Look."

Checking the doll over, she found a small white envelope tucked in its mouth. Inside were tickets for the ballet The Nutcracker *that Saturday night at the Academy of Music in Philadelphia.*

She couldn't believe it. "Can we afford it?"

"We can afford it, and besides that, you're worth it."

The birthday she had dreaded turned out to be her best one ever. Mike insisted she get a new dress and told her they would be having dinner at the Bellevue Stratford Hotel in Philadelphia before the show.

That Saturday, when they were dressing for their wonderful evening, she paraded around their bedroom in her new pink satin dress, hoping for Mike's approval.

Looking her over he smiled and said, "You look absolutely BE-U-TI-FUL!"

She remembered his arms around her; she remembered his kiss. He made her feel young again. She would never forget that birthday.

Rosemarie wiped her eyes, dumped the untouched cereal in the trash, and carried the dishes to the kitchen sink. When they were washed and back in the cabinet, she went down to the basement, put the laundry in the dryer, and commenced to dust the first floor before the girls came.

She always kept busy.

She was dusting the coffee table in the living room when she heard the lid of the mailbox rattle outside. Rushing to the front door, she opened it so fast that the mailman jumped aside. He pulled the blue woolen muffler from his face and said, "Wow, Rosemarie, I wasn't expecting you to open the door on a day like this."

"This weather doesn't bother me, Jack; I love snow. I've already been out in it. How are you doing? You must be cold. Can I get you a cup of hot coffee?"

"No, thanks. I'm fine. You got a load of mail today. What's going on?"

"It's my birthday."

"Well, happy birthday!"

Handing her a stack of letters, he asked, "You doing anything special today?"

"Yes, my daughters are taking me to André's for lunch."

"Isn't that the fancy French restaurant everybody's talking about?"

"Yes. I can't wait."

"Well, you're lucky the snow is supposed to stop soon. Have a good time."

"Thanks. I'm sure we will."

"You better get in, Rosemarie, before you get cold."

As Jack turned to leave, he noticed an envelope on the second step. "Wait a minute," he hollered. "There's a letter on the step. It must have slipped out of my hand." He bent over, picked up a large white envelope, and handed it to her. Rosemarie slid it under the others in her hand and closed the door.

Chapter 3

*H*urrying to the mahogany desk in the corner of the dining room, she located the silver letter opener in the top drawer and sat down to open the mail. Checking her watch, she figured she had plenty of time to read her birthday cards before the girls got there. She always called her daughters "girls." They were still girls to her, even though they were middle-aged moms themselves.

Bills and ads were tossed aside until only the cards remained. Time flew by as she became engrossed in each greeting and the notes that came with many of them. At last, she reached the large envelope at the bottom of the pile. Only then did she think to check her watch again—11:45. Not much time. She slit the flap and pulled out a pretty flowered card. Opening it, she expected to read it quickly and then get ready for her birthday lunch.

"God Loves You and So Do I," it read inside, but what followed sent shivers down her spine. Astonished, she muttered out loud, "Who in the world...?"

Minutes passed unnoticed as she pondered the card and then the envelope.

The doorbell rang; her head jerked up. She tried to make sense of the annoying noise. When the bell rang a second time, she came to life, suddenly realizing what it was. Pushing away from the desk, almost toppling her mahogany chair, she rushed into the living room, grasped the glass knob, and threw open the door.

Her two daughters stood there, stomping their booted feet. Anne, the older and taller of the two, was dressed in a long, tan, hooded coat that complimented her big, brown eyes and dark, wavy hair. Debbie, a striking blond with blue eyes, wore black slacks and a royal-blue jacket with a hat to match. Despite their winter outfits, both stood shivering in the cold.

"What took you so long to answer the door, Mother? We're freezing," Anne complained as the two of them swept past her into the warmth of the cozy living room.

Observing that there was no hat, coat, or handbag in sight, she blurted out, "How come you're not ready to go?"

"Something strange happened this morning," she answered. "Can we sit down for a minute?"

The sisters exchanged worried looks.

Opening her coat, Anne said, "All right." She scanned her mother from head to toe. She looked OK. Under an apron, she was wearing a soft, pink blouse and her new black pantsuit. Her pearl earrings and brown, salon-colored hair looked nice. What could be wrong?

Debbie, the nurse in the family, noticed the flushed cheeks and asked, "Don't you feel well, Mother?"

"I feel fine. Sit at the dining-room table. There's something I want you to see."

The mantel clock in the living room bonged twelve times as Debbie and Anne did as she asked.

"Will this take long, Mother?" Anne questioned. "We have reservations at André's at twelve thirty. We thought you were excited about going there for your birthday."

"I am. I am. This will only take a minute."

After the girls were seated, she placed the mysterious birthday card between them on the table.

"Take a look at this," she said.

At first glance the card looked innocent enough to both of them—"Happy Birthday" and a bouquet of pretty flowers on the outside. As they studied the inside, however, they could see some peculiarities. In place of a signature, a mysterious shape ✓ᴸ in black ink followed the greeting. Below that was a heart with the numbers 82/28 printed inside and an X on both sides.

Pointing to the humped shape, Debbie asked, "What's this?"

Rosemarie answered quietly, "It's shorthand for *I love you.*"

Anne's eyebrows shot up. Debbie's blue eyes popped as she said, "Really!"

"And in case you haven't figured it out, the numbers inside the heart are my age and birth date."

"And what about the Xs?" Anne asked. Not waiting for an answer, she said, "OK, I give up. Who sent it?"

"I have no idea. That's why I wanted you both to see it."

"Where's the envelope?" Debbie asked.

Standing behind the two of them, Rosemarie reached over to the desk for the envelope and placed it on the table where they all could see it. "That's a mystery too. Look at it!"

Addressed carefully in black, block print, the envelope had no return address or town of origin in the postmark.

"Wow, Mother! Are you trying to tell us you have an anonymous lover somewhere?" Debbie teased.

"For heaven's sake, no! It must be a joke."

Chapter 4

The mystifying card and envelope lay on Rosemarie's desk in the dining room for weeks into the New Year. When she sat there to pay bills or talk on the phone, it drew her like a magnet. Not a woman to waste time, she was annoyed with herself that she couldn't leave them alone. Time after time she reached for the pair, examining the envelope and every word on the card. The shorthand endearment intrigued her.

She racked her brain, seeking the identity of the sender. Who else would know shorthand—the Benn-Pitman style she learned in that dreaded Palmer Business School eons ago? Why use it now? Mike knew shorthand. He was her boss at the *Sentinel* newspaper in Philadelphia when they were dating, but Mike was gone. It couldn't be him, or could it? He always came up with unusual surprises for her birthday, and this looked like something he would do. Was this a message from beyond?

She smiled at the prospect. But if not Mike, who then?

Desperate one day, she called an old friend from her school days at Palmer.

"Lillian, this is Rosemarie Schafer."

"Rosemarie? It's so good to hear from you. For heaven's sake, how are you?"

"I'm fine, Lillian, but a bit frustrated at the moment, but I'm hoping you can help."

"What's going on?"

"Well, this is ridiculous, really ridiculous, but I received an odd card on my birthday a few weeks ago. There was no signature on it, just a Benn-Pitman shorthand form at the bottom of the card."

"*Shorthand!* Shorthand for what?" Lillian asked.

"For *I love you.*"

"*I love you.* Good heavens. And you don't know who sent it?"

"No, I was hoping you could suggest someone."

"Well, there weren't that many guys in Palmer with us. I don't even remember any of them, do you?"

"No."

"Could he be an old boyfriend from your working years?"

"No. I've thought about that. None of the fellas I dated back then knew shorthand except my husband, Mike, but he's been gone for several years now."

"Oh, I'm sorry, Rosemarie. How are you getting along?"

"I'm OK. I'm lonely, but I keep busy."

"Well, I'm sorry I can't help you. This is kind of exciting though, when you think about it. Who else our age is getting romantic mail from a mystery man? When you track this guy down, let me know who it is—will you?"

"OK, but I doubt I'll hear from him again."

By February the novelty of the card had worn off. Rosemarie put it back in the envelope and dropped it in the bottom drawer of her desk. She had too many other things in her life to waste any more time thinking about it.

The latest addition to her busy schedule was Bible study on Tuesday mornings from ten to twelve. Joan O'Malley, the leader of the newly formed group at Saint Mary's, caught up with her one day after church and asked her to join.

"I'd love to be part of the group," she told Joan, "but I'm embarrassed to tell you that I never really learned how to read the Bible."

"Don't worry," Joan said. "We'll all study the Bible together from page one. You'll learn how to read it, and we'll have discussions on the meanings of each chapter as we go along. You'll enjoy it."

Rosemarie joined the group but still had misgivings.

At the first meeting the following week, she noticed that most of the women were college graduates in their thirties and forties with young families. Singling Joan out when they took a break, she said, "Joan, I'm not sure I belong here. I'm a widow with a limited education and much older than the rest of the women. What can I contribute?"

"You're a great example of a Christian woman, Rosemarie," Joan said. "We can learn a lot from you. We're so happy to have you in our group." Joan hugged her, and that was the end of that. Tuesday-morning Bible study became a permanent fixture in her busy schedule. Week by week the age difference between her and the others disappeared until they were just a bunch of "girls" studying the Bible and becoming good friends.

Her daughters put the card on the back burner, too. Their lives were already on overload before the strange card arrived. Debbie was a single parent of three small children and a full-time nurse. She could hardly keep track of the essentials in her own life, much less ponder her mother's little mystery. Anne's thoughts were absorbed with the mounting bills for their four sons—three in college and one newly married. After the holidays she took a job as a receptionist in a doctor's office to help out.

The mysterious card issue faded until one year later.

Chapter 5

Rosemarie was both agitated and excited when she opened the mail on her next birthday. Another anonymous card! This time, it contained a clue about the sender. She was reading it for the third time when Anne called and sang, "Happy Birthday." When she finished, Rosemarie told her about the card.

"You have to be kidding, Mother!"

"I'm not kidding. I'm looking at it right now."

"Read it to me."

"The card is huge. It must have cost a fortune. It has two blue birds sitting in a dogwood tree on the front, a nice greeting inside, and then there's a note printed in red ink. *Keep healthy, happy, and contented, kid. I can call you kid because I am nine days older than you.* After that he wrote *I love you* again in shorthand. That really gets to me. What a nerve he has to sign the card like that and not let me know who he is. Apparently this character is my age, but that still doesn't ring any bells with me. The envelope is printed just like the last one, with no return address."

"How about the postmark?"

"Just numbers, no town. I can't imagine who he is."

"Me either, but I'm really curious now. To think, my mother really has a secret admirer. I love it! Wait till Debbie hears."

"Well, don't go telling the whole world about it. It could be embarrassing."

"Why *embarrassing?* Many a woman would be tickled to death to get that kind of mail."

"Well, if it is a joke, I don't want anyone thinking I believed it was for real. Somebody might be getting a big kick out of all of this and is just waiting to see my reaction."

"I don't think it's a joke. Let's think about it. He's probably someone you knew years ago. Are you sure you can't remember anyone from that business school you hated? That would be logical, since he used short-hand in both cards. Who else would know shorthand in this day and age?"

"That's what I have been trying to figure out. But the thing is there were only a few boys in my classes at Palmer, and I never became friendly with any of them. I was only there two semesters. Anyway, whoever he is, how would he know my birthday? I still think it is somebody playing a joke."

Anne thought, *If these birthday cards are being sent as some kind of joke, let the sender beware! Mother may be eighty-three, but she is not a confused, doddering old woman. Who else her age gets up every day at the crack of dawn, exercises for twenty minutes on the bedroom floor, then walks a mile to church? She's a bowler, a busy volunteer, and is sharp as a tack; she'll get to the bottom of this.*

Anne recalled a hilarious story about the way her mother treated a boyfriend when she was a teenager. According to her sister, Karla, she bit a young man who had the audacity to put his arm around her shoulders on their first date! Anne wondered what she would do to a man who was teasing her in her old age.

"But if he isn't a joker," Rosemarie continued, "then I can't think of even one man that I knew at any time in my life who would do some-thing like this."

"Maybe he's someone you met casually and didn't realize he took a liking to you."

"What do you mean?"

"Well, remember the time a year ago when I took you to the Cherry Hill Mall? You didn't feel like shopping that day, so you sat on a bench in the atrium and read while I went to Macy's. When I came back later, you were talking to a handsome white-haired gentleman who was sitting beside you."

"Oh, for heaven's sake, he was waiting for his wife and just wanted to talk."

"All right, but how about that time last summer when you were picnicking with Jim and me on the Delaware? A man came up to you when you were sitting on a swing and started talking to you. I remember because he must have noticed that you were with us. He came over to me and said he wanted to let me know that he was taking you for a walk along the river."

"Yes, I do remember that man. He was very nice. He said he used to walk along the river a lot with his wife in the summertime. She had died three months before, and he was lonely. When he saw me sitting by myself, he was hoping I would walk with him. That's all he wanted—just to walk. I don't even know his name."

"OK, but your mystery man could be somebody like those men. Maybe you only met him once or twice. You're not a bad-looking woman for your age, you know. Let's face it, you can still attract a man."

Rosemarie's face reddened. She laughed and said, "Boy, you really know how to flatter a girl."

"Well, it's true. You have a good figure, wear nice clothes, and color your hair. With all the things you're involved in, no one would guess your age. It's possible that some shy guy out there has his eye on you."

Their call ended a few minutes later with Rosemarie more disturbed than ever. She thought about their conversation off and on all day as she went about her Saturday chores. The next day, at Debbie's, when the dishes were cleared from her birthday party, the three of them hashed it over again but couldn't think of anyone who fit the picture of a mysterious romantic lover.

Rosemarie was baffled, but once again her busy schedule forced her to abandon the search for this man who was creating turmoil in her life.

By the end of January, the card and the envelope landed in the bottom drawer of her desk like the one before—out of sight but definitely not out of mind this time. The note became a niggling irritation that would not go away. Finally, she could keep her secret no longer. She couldn't resist telling the rest of the family, her bowling team, and the Bible study group about the mysterious cards. Everyone was hooked on her story immediately. Why not? If the note in the latest card could be believed, somewhere there was an eighty-three-year-old man behaving like a young Romeo!

Chapter 6

After Mass on the morning of her eighty-fourth birthday, Rosemarie went bowling with her team from church. The girls—great teasers—kept up a constant stream of speculation during all three games about the possibility of her receiving another card from her Phantom Romeo. It was impossible for her to concentrate. She bowled her lowest score of the year and arrived home nervous as a schoolgirl to await the arrival of the mail. When it came, she stood at the front door and shuffled through the pile until she spotted an envelope with the familiar block printing. Her heart leapt as she read the postmark: Cape May, New Jersey. Dropping everything else on the tea table, she sat on the love seat next to the door and tore open the envelope.

The outside of the card, printed in gold script on heavy, cream-colored stock, read:

People born in the magical month of December
Add a sparkle to life
And are a joy to remember.

Inside, hand-printed in red ink, it read:

Dec. 28, 1994

Dear Rosemarie,
Ever since 1926 I have considered you my "first love." You may have forgotten me completely. If so, I understand. Perhaps we will meet again-probably in our next life.
   Until then: "au revoir."

Chapter 7

1926…1926…I was seventeen. Where was I?

Rosemarie's mind raced. Unhappy memories bubbled up from the past.

By 1926 Prohibition had changed her family's lifestyle dramatically. Pop, a German immigrant and once the proud proprietor of Schafer's Saloon and Dining Room in downtown Philadelphia, had been reduced in status to night watchman in a hat factory. By the stroke of a pen in 1920, his popular establishment—the first in the city to have tiled floors and a mahogany bar with brass rails—was shuttered. His customers—businessmen, theater folk, and politicians, including the mayor—were gone. Loyal to his new country, he would not defy the law as others did, so he lost everything. Limited by his broken English, he had few choices for employment. Night watchman was all he could get.

The heydays of her childhood had vanished overnight. Everything that she, her older sister, Karla, and her two little brothers, Stevie and Joey, had enjoyed—the expensive toys, private school, fancy clothes, and their pony—all were gone, quickly replaced by hardship. Even now, it riled her. Only by the ingenuity of Mom did their family survive. She remembered the sacrifices—remembering clearly the day in 1926 when her own dream for the future was shattered.

In her mind's eye, she could see Mom and Pop coming into the kitchen that night in January just as she and Karla finished the dishes.

"Karla, take the boys upstairs and help them with their homework," Mom had said. "Dad and I want to talk with Rosemarie."

Rosemarie stood rooted to the floor, wondering what was coming next. When her siblings were out of earshot, the three of them sat at the kitchen table. Mom, in a flowered housedress she had made herself, looked small and tired. Her hair, pulled tight in a knot at the nape of her neck, seemed grayer than before, and Pop—a giant of a man—looked solemn as a judge. His shock of white hair and curled, white mustache made a stark contrast to the dark-blue work shirt covering his huge, barrel chest.

Mom started. "Pop and I have talked it over, and we think it would be best if you left high school in April and finished your education at Palmer Business School in center city, like Karla did last year."

Blood rose to her face as she heard the words.

Pop sat silent as Mom went on in a cheerful tone. "Palmer will give you good preparation for a job, Rosemarie. You see how well Karla made out after six months at Palmer. She is so happy with her secretarial position at Sears and Roebuck. She loves getting dressed up every day for work. You will, too. We'd like you to try Palmer. The spring semester starts after Easter."

Hot tears rolled down her cheeks. Hands clenched under the table, she responded angrily, "I don't care about getting dressed up, and I don't want to be a secretary like Karla. I want to be a nurse. I want to take care of people. That's what I have been dreaming of ever since seventh grade. To sit every day in a stuffy office typing and taking shorthand would be like going to jail for me!"

Pop got up from his chair. Head down, he left the room without a word.

"I'm sorry, Rosemarie," Mom said, her own eyes brimming with tears. "The fact of the matter is we need another salary to keep the house going. We can't wait until you finish high school and graduate from nursing school. Your brothers are growing fast, and even with Karla's paycheck added to Pop's, there's not enough to pay our bills."

Rosemarie sat in stunned silence. Finally, she spoke up. "All right, Mom. I'll go to Palmer. I'm sorry, I didn't understand."

Later that evening, in the tiny bedroom they shared, Rosemarie and Karla whispered back and forth. They couldn't believe things had gotten this bad. Both of them had memories of their family life when times were good.

"Karla, I miss our big three-story house on Broad Street and Pop's Saloon, don't you?" Rosemarie asked.

"I sure do. It was Prohibition that caused all this trouble. When the government passed that law, making it illegal to sell alcohol, Pop lost it all. Wasn't it awful when we had to move to that first rented row house and we cried for weeks when we had to leave Saint John's Academy and go to a public school?"

"I'll never forget it," Rosemarie said. "We didn't know anybody in the new school, and I missed my friends so much, but leaving high school now and having to go to business school is worse. If only Pop hadn't lost the saloon." Rosemarie sniffled. "I can handle living in a row house, and wearing hand-me-down and homemade clothes, but giving up my plans of becoming a nurse and being chained to a desk for the rest of my life is almost more than I can bear." She sobbed noisily.

"Shhhhh, it's OK. It's OK," Karla whispered. "It will all work out somehow. I know this is going to be hard for you, but just think how terrible it must be for Pop to work in a hat factory after being the owner of "Schafer's Saloon."

The memories left her sad.

Rosemarie looked at the birthday card once more. She was back in the moment with her mystery man. She hated to admit it, but she felt a flutter of excitement as she reread the astonishing message.

"How could he say he loved me since 1926? I don't even remember dating anyone then."

Nothing made sense.

Chapter 8

When Rosemarie read the outrageous message over the phone to Anne and Debbie that evening, they were shocked. Anne insisted they start a serious investigation into the matter, and she agreed. The anonymous card business had been fascinating up until now, but the testimony of this man's love for her in this last card was over the top. How could he possibly write such a thing and not let her know who he was?

The more Rosemarie thought about it, the more she felt this man wanted her to find him. The girls thought so too. This last card, postmarked Cape May, was the best clue yet. Even so, it brought her no closer to discovering his identity. She didn't know any men in Cape May. Was this some kind of a game for him?

Anne thought they should contact her oldest son, Matt, and his wife, Kate, for help. Kate, a teacher, was a master at research and had recently compiled a family history back several hundred years; and Matt, a computer whiz, could get all kinds of information from the Internet.

"Maybe between the two of them, they could put the clues together and come up with an answer, Mother. What do you think?"

"I'm at my wit's end," Rosemarie said. "Could you call them tonight? This whole thing is driving me crazy."

Anne called Matt right after she hung up but got nowhere. He was away on a business trip, and Kate, though interested, was sick with a virus. She said she would call back when Matt got home and they had a chance to talk about it.

There was nothing for Rosemarie to do but wait and wonder.

Chapter 9

The next Tuesday, the ladies in her Bible-study group went bananas when Rosemarie fed them the latest chapter in her love story. Fortunately, she did not tell them a word until coffee break. Their Bibles lay unopened after that. The discussion on Kings, chapter 4, verse 10, which was to take place after coffee, was shelved by mutual consent until the following week so the mystery of Rosemarie's secret lover could be completely hashed over. The thirty-somethings, whose lives were filled with such mundane things as babysitter woes and soccer games, were suddenly thrust into the real-life love affair of their own octogenarian member. Everyone had an opinion, everyone was excited, and they weren't the only ones. Ever since the second card when Rosemarie started telling others about her mysterious Romeo, people were anxious to hear the latest happening in her romantic story. Due to her age and the nature of the cards, the people she told about them told others. By the time the third card arrived with its declaration of love, there was an extensive group of people following the story from all over—including the three college campuses of her grandsons.

Overnight, her annual mystery in the mail had morphed into a sizzling senior soap opera, yet still Romeo remained in the shadows.

Chapter 10

A call from Anne in mid-February changed everything. In an instant Romeo was out of the limelight.

"Guess what? I'm going to be a grandmom!" Anne announced.

Rosemarie squealed. "I can't believe it! When did you hear the news?"

"This morning. The doorbell rang around ten o'clock, and when I opened the door, there stood Matt and Kate grinning like Cheshire cats. As soon as they got in the house, they told Jim and me they were expecting. The four of us stood there in the living room, hugging and laughing and crying like a bunch of idiots."

Tears of happiness spilled from her eyes as Rosemarie asked, "When's the baby due?"

"In September."

"Great! We'll have a lot to do between now and then. I want to embroider my first great-grandchild a quilt for the cradle, just like I did for his father."

"Is it a boy or a girl?"

"They want to be surprised."

"That's OK. I like surprises. Would you mind if I have the shower?"

"Whoa, Mother. You're going too fast for me. I'm still getting used to the idea of being a grandmom. I haven't even thought about a shower."

"Well, let me do it. You girls are working, and I love to entertain. I haven't had a party since your dad died. This is going to be fun!"

Still floating on air Monday afternoon, Rosemarie walked to the craft shop downtown and bought a baby quilt to embroider with a big, brown teddy bear in the middle. At home, she dislodged the embroidery hoop and needles from her bedroom closet and got to work. Humming as she sewed, her mind filled with dreams of her first great-grandchild. She imagined the baby sleeping under this quilt in the maple cradle his father had slept in. She pictured the tiny infant on her shoulder, asleep in her arms, dozing off in a stroller she was pushing in the park. Yet even so, every once in a while her Phantom Romeo intruded.

Ever since 1926 you were my first love. How could she forget those words? With all of the excitement over the baby, she never thought to ask Anne if Matt and Kate had decided to help her find him. Considering that her secret lover was probably the furthest thing from their minds right now, she decided to wait for a while and then ask them herself.

Chapter 11

By early April Rosemarie could wait no longer. She invited Matt and Kate for dinner one Sunday afternoon. As they were finishing dessert, she blurted out, "I know you two have a lot on your mind right now, but I don't know where else to turn. Do you think you could help me find the man who has been sending me those anonymous birthday cards? Your mom and Aunt Debbie and I have been trying to figure out who he is for three years now, and we haven't gotten anywhere."

"I'd love to help," Kate said. "Sorry—I meant to get back to you when Mom first asked us before. I guess we got distracted."

Matt chuckled. "We're getting used to the idea of becoming parents now. I'd be glad to help, too. What do you want us to do?"

"Thanks! That's a relief. I'm going let you read the cards first. Maybe you can pick up something from the clues he gives. I haven't had any luck."

Getting up from the table, she went over to her desk and withdrew three envelopes from the bottom right-hand drawer and placed them on the table.

"I know you two have heard all about these, but up until now no one else but your mom and Aunt Debbie have seen them."

"This is awesome," Kate said. "It's all so romantic. I can't wait to look at them."

"Well, go ahead. See if you get any ideas."

Rosemarie pulled a new spiral notebook and a pen from the desk and placed them on the table near the cards. "You'll probably want to take notes. Be sure to check out the envelopes, too."

"I love doing this kind of stuff," Kate said as she picked up the first envelope dated December 27, 1994. "Thanks for letting us in on this."

Rosemarie left them poring over the cards and envelopes. As she cleared the table and began doing the dishes, she wondered if she made the right decision allowing her grandson and his wife to see this intimate correspondence from her secret lover. It was all so absurd. What would they think?

Chapter 12

Matt called a few days later. He and Kate had come up with a plan on how to proceed with their investigation. They had discussed the cards with Anne, and all of them felt that the mystery man had some connection to the Palmer Business School she had attended. Matt had already gleaned some preliminary facts on the school from the Internet.

"When you went there, Grandmom, the school was located on the second floor of the Mercantile Library on Eighth Street in Philadelphia, but that place is no longer there. All the records from Palmer were moved to the Free Library in downtown Philly a while back. After Easter, Kate's going to take a day off and do some more research there. She wants to get information on their graduations—and especially the names of the graduates for 1926. Maybe one of the boys' names will ring a bell. What do you think?"

"It's worth a try, but as I told your mom, there were only a few boys, and I didn't get to know any of them. But after all, we have to start somewhere. I say keep going. It's so nice of Kate to take time off work to do this."

"She doesn't mind at all. In fact, she's really pepped up about trying to find this guy. I'm getting a kick out of it, too. I want to see what kind of a man comes up with this once-a-year romantic deal. Don't expect immediate results, though. Research takes time. It may be a while before we get any concrete information."

"At least somebody's doing something. I can't get that last card out of my mind. All this time I thought it was somebody playing a joke, but

I don't think that anyone would go so far as to say he loved me way back then, do you?"

"No. I think it's for real. Everyone who knows about your Phantom Romeo can't wait to see who he is, including us. We'll find him somehow. You can count on it!"

Chapter 13

$\mathcal{M}$att was right; the detective work did take a long time. Kate didn't call until mid-May.

"Sorry, I couldn't get back to you sooner, Grandmom. We've had a shortage of substitute teachers at school, and I couldn't take a day off until yesterday."

"That's OK, Kate. I'm just happy you are working on it. Did you find anything?"

"Not much. I spent all day at the Free Library in Philadelphia, but I only found two references connected to Palmer Business School. The first was an ad for the school in the Stanton Theatre Program for the week of February 18, 1924, and the other was a Benn-Pitman shorthand book from the 1920s stamped with the school's name. The man who helped me suggested that I contact the Atwater Kent Museum in Philly for more information.

"The problem is the time frame. It being so long ago, it's hard to track records back that far. I'll keep trying, though. I'm hoping we will come across an old Palmer yearbook or maybe even a newspaper clipping about their graduations.

"I'm keeping track of everything we already know about your mystery man in that notebook you gave us, and now I'm adding whatever I can find on the school. Matt called the post office, too, and found that they usually don't handstamp regular mail unless someone makes a special request. Looks like this man made a real effort to keep his whereabouts secret in the beginning, but that last card with a Cape May postmark is a real break in the case.

"We'll find him, Grandmom. It may take a while, but we'll find him."

Rosemarie was happy that Kate was not giving up but disappointed with her report. The mystery had to be solved soon. Time was running out for Kate's participation.

Chapter 14

The next report on the investigation came on the Fourth of July at a family picnic in Anne's backyard. Kate came over to Rosemarie as soon as she arrived.

"I want to let you know how my research is going on the Palmer Business School, Grandmom."

Rosemarie hugged her and said, "I've been anxious to hear about it, Kate, but I didn't want to bother you. How are you feeling?"

"I feel great! The baby is moving around a lot now, and Matt and I are getting excited. We only have a few months to go."

"The last six weeks at work were so busy I didn't get a chance to do any research, but when school closed, I contacted the Atwater Kent Museum in Philly. A woman on the staff agreed to do a search for Palmer Business School, but the next day she called and said she couldn't find a thing. She told me to contact the Archives Department of the *Philadelphia Inquirer*. That's the only newspaper left in the city that was around in the 1920s. She thought they might have news articles about school graduations from the '20s. I called the paper right away and talked to the man in charge. That was another dead end. He said all of their records prior to 1940 had been transferred to the Urban Archives at Temple University six months ago. He was nice enough to give me their telephone number, so I contacted them next.

"A girl named Dorothy—probably a student—answered. I told her the basics of your story and what I was looking for. She loved hearing about the birthday cards from your mystery man and wanted to help but warned me that Temple is still organizing the material they received from the *Inquirer*, so she won't have any information anytime soon. She took my name and address and assured me that if she finds anything about Palmer's graduations, she'll make copies of the articles and mail them to me. I'm really excited. Matt will take over the search from there on the Internet. We're finally getting somewhere!"

"Kate, I appreciate everything you and Matt are doing. It all sounds so complicated to me with all those phone calls."

"That's the way research is, Grandmom. You have to be patient and persistent. I love digging for something, especially if you eventually find what you're looking for."

Rosemarie admired Kate's determination, but she thought she and Matt were wasting their time. She was more inclined to go along with Anne's suggestion that her mystery man was someone she might have met casually somewhere—maybe even in Haddonfield, but who could he be?

Chapter 15

The inquiry into Romeo's identity took a back seat as summer wore on. Rosemarie got caught up in a whirlwind of activities: first, a neighborhood picnic three houses down at the Fosters'; then the family reunion at her nephew Paul's house in Doylestown, Pennsylvania; and finally, she started planning for Kate's baby shower.

Anne wanted to make pink and blue table favors, and Debbie offered to send the invitations, but the menu and all the fancy stuff were left to her. She loved to entertain. Thinking that at her age she might not have an opportunity to host a shower again, Rosemarie took great delight in figuring out every detail. After many hours poring through her magazines and recipes, she finally decided on a simple but elegant menu. She would serve a colorful variety of cut-up fruit and three kinds of cheeses and fancy crackers on doily-covered glass platters while Kate opened her gifts. The lunch would consist of fancy tea sandwiches on silver trays, a strawberry salad in her big crystal bowl, and iced tea in her stemmed crystal glasses. The dessert—a family favorite—her butter pound cake, decorated with pink and blue icing, would sit on her pedestalled crystal cake plate.

She would dress the dining-room table with a pink linen cloth, overlaid with her finest lace table cover, and use the china luncheon dishes with tiny pink and blue flowers around the edge. Her silver flatware with embossed roses would have to be polished, but she knew they would look lovely next to pink, linen napkins.

When Anne heard her plans, she laughed and asked, "You're not hoping for a girl, are you, Mother?"

"I'll be happy with a boy or a girl. Why?"

"Your color scheme sounds mostly pink to me."

"Uh oh. You're right. I'll fix that."

The next day she searched every box in the attic until she found the beautiful blue china cradle that Mike had sent to her at Anne's birth. Back then it had been filled with her favorite flowers—tiny, pink roses. This time it would serve nicely as the centerpiece of her table filled with baby pink, white, and blue carnations. Mike would be pleased.

On the third Sunday in August, the day of the shower, everything went perfectly—just as she imagined. Everyone was having a good time; the gifts had been opened and lunch had been served. Kate was so happy with everything. Then, suddenly, she pushed away from the table.

Anne jumped up and went over to her. "Are you OK?"

Kate smiled weakly and said, "I think I'm having labor pains, but I'm not due for three weeks."

Someone called Matt. Every mother at the shower sympathized and comforted Kate until he arrived. The party was over for Kate, but the excited group of ladies who remained stayed on, chattering, eating cake, and hoping to hear good news before they left. By five o'clock they gave up and went home. Rosemarie was exhausted, worried, and thrilled—all at the same time.

Nine hours later, Great-Grandson Bryan made his appearance, but her Phantom Romeo remained in hiding.

Chapter 16

*F*our months flew by. Bryan was christened. Thanksgiving and Christmas came and went. Rosemarie was on edge when her birthday rolled around. She wondered, after the shocking birthday card last year, what her mysterious lover would do this time. The mailman came early that day, but for the first time in four years, there was no big envelope with black, block print—no romantic card signed in shorthand.

She didn't know what to think. Was her secret admirer tired of his game—or worse yet, since he was up in years like her, did he die? Suddenly, she felt old, abandoned, and dispirited. She hadn't realized how much those cards meant to her. It had been fun thinking about love and romance again. She especially liked the attention she received at family gatherings and at church when someone would ask, "How's your love life, Rosemarie?" This man, whoever he was, made her feel like a young woman again. She liked that feeling. She wanted to know who he was. She wanted to meet him and ask him why he sent her those cards. Now what? The whole magic dream seemed to be fading away. Even Matt and Kate were discouraged. They hadn't heard a word from the Archive Department at Temple University.

Chapter 17

One Saturday in late January, a large, brown envelope from Temple University arrived in Matt and Kate's mailbox. Inside they found copies of news articles published in the *Philadelphia Inquirer* concerning all Palmer Business School graduations from 1926 through 1930. The graduates from each year were listed just as Kate had hoped. There were only ten boys shown for the year 1926. Matt checked, using the computer, to see if any of those names were listed in the Cape May telephone directory.

There was one. Charles Benson.

"How can we be absolutely sure he is our man?" Matt asked.

"There is only one way," Kate said.

Monday morning she contacted the Bureau of Vital Statistics in Philadelphia. They agreed to her request.

Two weeks later the mailman slipped another brown envelope into their mailbox. The key to Grandmom's mystery was inside.

Kate squealed when she read the contents. Matt came running from the baby's room. "What's the matter?"

Waving the paper in her hand, she said, "This is it. Charles Benson was born December nineteenth, nine days before Grandmom. He's our man! Should we call her?"

"Let Mom tell her. I know she'll want to hear Grandmom's reaction."

Kate called Anne immediately.

"We found him!" she exulted. She gave Anne the information that confirmed Romeo's identity.

"Great job, Kate! Did you tell Grandmom yet?"

"No, we thought you'd like to do that."

"Oh, I do. I do. Thanks for letting me be the bearer of good news. This is so exciting. I'll call her right away."

Chapter 18

Rosemarie's phone rang insistently at dinnertime that Saturday night. She stirred the beef stew, turned the heat down, and finally picked up the call on the third ring.

"Matt and Kate found your mystery man!" Anne trilled.

"You're kidding. For heaven's sake, who is he?"

"Are you ready for this? It's Charles Benson!"

"Charles Benson? I never heard of him."

"He is definitely your man, Mother. He graduated from Palmer in June 1926, was born nine days before you, and he lives in Cape May!"

"Well, how can that be? The name means nothing to me. I don't understand this whole thing. After all this time, and all the detective work Matt and Kate did, and now they come up with a man they are absolutely sure is my Romeo, and I don't know him at all. Now what?"

"Well, we have his name and address. Let's go down to Cape May tomorrow and confront him. We can't keep going on like this."

"Anne, I don't think that's a good idea. It's been over a year since I heard from him. Maybe he's lost interest—or maybe he's dead."

"Well, if he's dead, then that will be the end of it, but if he's there, we'll at least find out what this card business was all about."

"I don't want to go."

"OK. I'll take Jim along. He'd like to meet the man anyway."

"Call me as soon as you get home, will you? I don't know this Charles Benson, but I'd like to know how he knows so much about me."

Chapter 19

Rosemarie was as nervous as a wet hen all day Sunday. She could barely concentrate at Mass in the morning, and by noon she was a wreck. She called Debbie and together they talked over all that Anne had told them about the results of Matt and Kate's detective work. They tried to imagine what would happen if Anne met up with Charles Benson in Cape May. Would he be surprised that she found him, or did he expect to be discovered? How would he explain the three-year correspondence with a woman who did not know him?

The two of them came up with all kinds of scenarios before their call ended, but nothing seemed logical.

By dinnertime Rosemarie had made a batch of cookies for Matt and Kate, ironed everything in her ironing basket, and had nothing left to do but heat up the leftover stew from the day before.

Then the phone rang.

"You better sit down, Mother," Anne said.

"Why?"

"I have an incredible story to tell you. Did you eat dinner yet?"

"No. I was just going to start."

"This is going to take a while. Maybe you better eat and call me back."

"Are you kidding? I couldn't eat a thing now. What happened?"

"Well, first of all, Romeo wasn't home when we got there. On the way down, I figured out what I was going to say, and when we reached his home, I got right out of the car, went up to the door, and rang the bell. No one came to the door. I rang twice more. Nothing."

"What kind of a house was it?"

"It was a cute little white bungalow with blue shutters, not far from the bay."

"OK. Go on."

"It took us an hour and a half to get there, and Jim was ready to call it quits when no one answered the door, but there was no way I was going to give up that easily after all the work Matt and Kate did to find him. I wanted to go right home and call Matt to see if he could get me Mr. Benson's telephone number, but Jim insisted we stop at the Lobster House for lunch to make the trip worthwhile. We didn't get home until after three, but the minute we got in, I called Matt. Thank heavens he was home. I told him what I wanted. He got off the phone, went to his computer, and in a few minutes he gave me the number. Believe me, my heart was pumping. I hung up from Matt and dialed the number right away."

"You really have nerve, Anne. I don't think I could just call the man like that."

"Well, I knew we were getting close to finding him, and my adrenaline was pumping furiously.

"The phone rang and rang. I was just about to hang up when a man answered. I asked him if he was Charles Benson. He said, 'Yes, I'm Charles.' I'm telling you I had chills running up and down my spine."

"What did you say next?"

"I told him I wasn't sure if he was the man I was looking for. I said, 'The Charles Benson I'm trying to find knew someone with the last name of Schafer from Philadelphia.' He didn't answer right away, but after a while, he said, 'I knew a young woman with that last name, but that was a long time ago.'"

"I don't believe this."

"Believe it, Mother. Wait until you hear the rest."

"What did you say when he said he knew someone with the name of Schafer?"

"I told him my name and said that I was your daughter and then I asked him how he knew you."

"Anne, this is like something out of a movie."

"That's exactly what I was thinking. He talked slowly, but he seemed prepared as if he expected someone to call. He said, 'I met Rosemarie at Palmer Business School in Philadelphia when we were both seventeen.' And then I could just about hear him when he said, 'And I fell in love with her.'"

"What!"

"I know, I know. I told him that was impossible. I said we gave you his name and you didn't recognize him at all.

"Then he said, 'I never spoke a word to her. She was so beautiful, and I was very shy.'"

Rosemarie was flabbergasted. This man had fallen in love with her when she was seventeen, and now seventy years later he was still thinking about her? Unbelievable! How could it be?

Anne went on. "He told me he could remember the first time he ever saw you. He wanted to tell me the whole story. So I just listened."

Chapter 20

Charles began, "I know this might be hard for you to believe, Anne, since it was so long ago, but I remember the first time I saw your mother, as though it was yesterday. It was April twelfth, 1926—my first day at Palmer Business School.

"I lived in North Philly at the time and had to take a trolley into center city that morning. The ride took about a half hour, and the whole way I kept hoping that I'd have better luck with girls at this school than I did at Frankford High. My dating record up to that point was nil, but I already knew the odds were in my favor. My sister, Harriet, graduated from Palmer the previous June, and although I never dreamed then that I would be going there, myself, I took note that there were plenty of good-looking girls and not many guys in her class. As fate would have it, a long bout with scarlet fever in my senior year ruined my chances of graduating, so instead of repeating the year at Frankford, I decided to take some business courses at Palmer in the spring.

"That first day things were just as I expected—lots of girls, only a few guys. Typing was my first class. I took a seat in the last row to get a good look at the rest of the students as they entered. A bunch of girls gathered at the front of the room to talk. One of them, a pretty young lady in a pink sweater, caught my eye. That was your mother, Anne. Quieter than the others, she had dark, wavy hair and big, brown eyes. She seemed unhappy about something, but even so, she was beautiful, very beautiful—just the kind of girl I always wanted to date.

"As the weeks went by, I really fell for her. I wanted to ask her for a date, but I could never get up enough nerve. It was that way the whole semester. I guess I figured a skinny guy like me—with straight hair and glasses—wouldn't have a chance with a girl like her.

"When the second semester started in the fall, Rosemarie didn't return to classes. By then, I worked in the office at school and heard that she had taken a job during the day and transferred to Palmer's night school, so I decided to do the same thing. I got a job at the Bourse Building at Fifth and Market during the day and started night school at Palmer. Lucky me! I was assigned to sit in the row right behind her in Stenography class.

"I used to spend hours daydreaming about her. I would imagine the dates we would have—movies on Friday nights at the Strand, dancing on Saturday evenings at the Starlight Ballroom, and picnics on Sunday afternoons in Fairmount Park. I would shower her with gifts of flowers and chocolates and slip love poems into her steno book. But none of it ever happened. I never said a word to her. The months went by, and the next thing I knew, it was graduation.

"Rosemarie looked so pretty that day in a pink taffeta dress. After graduation, there was a dance. I was standing at one end of the hall near the dance floor when Rosemarie danced by with another girl. I'll never forget the look on her face as she went by. She looked me right in the eye, and it seemed to me that she was pleading silently, 'Charles, please ask me to dance.' But I couldn't. I didn't know how to dance. I was afraid. I guess I was a coward. Anyhow, I was miserable. I figured that would probably be the last time I'd ever see her.

"But I was wrong. A year later, I was walking up Market Street, heading back to the office after lunch, when I spotted Rosemarie coming down the other side of the street. She looked gorgeous in a rose-colored suit, with one of those cloche hats all the girls were wearing at the time. I watched her enter the Pennsylvania Furniture Company and wasn't sure if she was shopping or working there. So, the next day I took an early lunch, went into the store, and saw her typing in the back office. That did it! I wasn't going to lose her this time. I decided to catch up with her one day when she left work and introduce myself.

"It took me a month to get up the courage, but finally, one afternoon, I left work early and hot-footed it down to the Pennsylvania Furniture Company. I was dressed in my best suit, higher than a kite, as I waited for the store to empty at five o'clock. But by five fifteen, everyone was out, the owner locked up, and there was no sign of Rosemarie. I waited a few days and tried again. She wasn't there that time, either. I had to find out what was going on, so I asked the owner if Rosemarie was on vacation. He said she had taken another job, but he wouldn't tell me where.

"I lost track of her after that."

Chapter 21

Rosemarie sat in shock long after Anne hung up, trying to digest everything Charles Benson had revealed to her. His story seemed preposterous, yet it must be true. Who would make up something like that? He even remembered the color of her graduation dress! She smiled as she thought of his words to Anne, *"...and I fell in love with her."* A tingle of excitement ran through her. For a moment she felt like a teenage girl once again. To think that he would write those words first to her and then say them again to Anne more than seventy years after he had those feelings seemed beyond belief.

Anne said he told her that he had been married for over fifty years and had a son and a daughter. His wife died six years ago, and since then he had been very lonely. In the last few years, he began listening to his old records in the evening to pass the time. One song, "When You and I Were Seventeen," reminded him of his first experience of falling in love. That's when he got the wild idea of trying to find her.

She laughed. It was a wild idea. With the two of them in their eighties, what did he think he was going to do if he did find her? This Charles Benson is definitely a character. *He must have a good memory, though, if he can remember me from that far back.*

Charles was clever, too. According to Anne, he searched a Philadelphia telephone directory for her maiden name to see if any of her relatives were still in the area. He found four and called everyone with no success until he reached Steve's son, Dan. When Dan heard Charles's story—that he was a childhood friend of hers visiting the city and wanted to surprise her with a visit—he gave him her married name and address in New Jersey.

Rosemarie pondered what Anne told her next. "That's when the birthday card business started, Mother. When he brought that up, I stopped him and reminded him that he said he never spoke to you. How could he know your birthday? His explanation was that even though he lost track of you, he still thought about you often. Apparently, he didn't have a girlfriend when he was sent overseas with the army, so he continued to daydream about you. I guess you were a fantasy of his—kind of his pinup girl for the six years he served. When he came home, he went to city hall in Philly to see if you were still single. That's when he discovered your birthday and that you were married."

Rosemarie smiled to herself at Anne's pinup-girl remark. She always could tell a good story, and Charles certainly did give her enough far-fetched material to work with.

"He wanted to know how you were and if your hair was still brown," Anne said with a laugh. "He also asked if I thought you would speak to him."

"I don't remember him at all, Anne. Isn't that sad? Maybe I'll call him. Do you have his number?"

Anne was floored.

Chapter 22

Rosemarie wavered back and forth about calling Charles. The ball was in her court now. Anne did not give him her telephone number.

What to do? Did she want to encourage him by calling, or should she leave things as they were? She already had a busy life, chock-full of activities, but no romance. Charles was definitely a romantic. It might be fun to get to know this man who said he loved her so long ago. Maybe they could go out to dinner or to a movie sometime. The practical side of her argued, *Are you out of your mind even thinking about dating again? He might not be in good health. What's the point of starting anything at your age?* On the other hand, she asked herself, *Why not? What do I have to lose?*

The more she thought about it, the more she felt she should, at the very least, talk to Charles. She had to get used to thinking about her Phantom Romeo as a real man named Charles.

Monday morning, in between games, she ran the whole episode of Anne's talk with Charles and her own indecision about what to do next past the bowling team. They lost all three games but agreed unanimously that she should contact Charles. The Bible study group on Tuesday felt the same. Everyone in both groups was thrilled with the latest news and could barely wait to see what would happen next.

Rosemarie sat at her desk in the dining room Tuesday afternoon, twisting the telephone cord, picking the phone up, then putting it down. Finally, she raised the receiver to her ear, dialed quickly, and then held her breath until a man answered.

"Charles?" she asked in a shaky voice.

"Yes."

"This is Rosemarie."

"Rosemarie! How are you?"

"I'm fine. My daughter said you would like to talk with me."

"Yes, I certainly would. It's so nice of you to call. I would have called you, but your daughter didn't want to give me your number until she talked with you. I understand. It's been a long time. I wasn't sure you would remember me from Palmer."

"I didn't. That's why I was stumped with that last birthday card when you mentioned knowing me since 1926. I remembered that I was attending Palmer at that time, but I didn't remember getting to know any of the boys in my class. I was only in day school one semester, then I had to go to work and attend school at night."

"I know. That's when I changed to night school, too."

"My daughter told me that. I can't believe it."

"Well, it's true. I had a serious crush on you, you know. I ended up sitting right behind you in Stenography class."

"I can't picture you. How can you remember me after all this time?"

"Why not? You were my first love."

"And to think I never knew it."

"I know. I was a dumb kid back then. We have a lot of catching up to do. What have you been doing all these years?"

Rosemarie laughed. "Where do I start?"

"Wherever you want."

"Well, as you know, I married during the war, had two beautiful daughters, moved to New Jersey, and then…"

Time flew by as she told the highlights of her life to this man she did not know and then listened as he shared some of his lifetime memories with her. They talked about their days at Palmer, the Philadelphia where they grew up, the Vaudeville shows, and the first movies. Their conversation went on and on until finally Charles, conscious of the fact that she called him and the toll was getting higher by the minute, ended the conversation.

"Well, we've had a good, long chat, Rosemarie. Are you sure you don't remember me now?"

"I'm sorry, Charles, I don't. But I did enjoy talking with you."

"I enjoyed our chat too, Rosemarie. Maybe we can get together sometime."

"That would be nice."

"Good. I'll call you next time."

Chapter 23

Two weeks later, Charles kept his promise. Rosemarie had but-
terflies in her stomach when she heard his voice. With great
enthusiasm she said, "Charles, I'm so glad to hear from you again." She
expected him to echo her feelings and thought that their conversation
would be somewhat like the first, with more reminiscing and perhaps a
request for a date this time.

When his first words were "I'm sorry, Rosemarie," her heart sank.
He continued in a solemn tone. "There's a problem in my family that
requires my attention right now." He coughed and cleared his throat.
"So I won't be able to make a date for us to meet anytime soon." His
excuse sounded hollow and false. She felt rejected at once. The more
he tried to explain, the worse things got until finally he said in closing,
"When things straighten out, I'll call you."

Rosemarie was stunned. Her fairy-tale romance was over, but why?
What did she do?

After agonizing all day, she reviewed the call with Anne later that
evening. "I must have said something in that first call that turned him
off, but I can't imagine what it was. All we talked about was the time we
spent at Palmer and what we've been doing since then. He sounded fine
when we hung up."

Anne had no answers but suggested that Charles might really have
some trouble in his family. She was certain he would call again.

Rosemarie didn't agree. He gave her the brush-off. That's all there
was to it.

Chapter 24

This unexpected turn of events was more than a disappointment to Rosemarie. As she thought back over the last four years, she realized that bit by bit, year by year, her persistent and elusive Romeo had roped her in, teasing her with mystique and luring her with words until she was convinced that romance could once again be part of her life. Now, after all that, this Charles Benson, her unmasked Phantom, was backing off. To make matters worse, everyone she knew was hooked on her bizarre love story. What could she tell them? That she had been ditched? Never!

She determined that no one but Anne and Debbie would hear about the second call and swore them to secrecy. They all agreed that as slow as this man operated, no one would be surprised if it took him another year to make the next move.

Over the winter she tried to figure out what made the fire in her Romeo fizzle. Had his children discouraged him from starting a relationship this late in life? Had he decided to keep his fantasy of meeting her just that—a fantasy? Maybe he never even considered meeting her at all until he was found. Still, if he didn't want her to find him, why did he put those clues in the last two cards?

Back and forth she went as the cold dreary months wore on with no word from Charles. By spring, she felt let down and frustrated. She decided to stir the pot a bit by sending Charles an Easter card with a little note, but there was no response.

In June, she watched a TV show about couples who had known each other in their youth and had finally gotten together in their later years. The show reminded her of her situation with Charles. It burned her up. She was not going to let him get away scot-free. No way.

Immediately after the show, she sat down at her desk and fired off a heated letter to him. Fortunately, she thought to call Anne before she mailed it. The gist of it was, "You have no right to drop me after you got me interested. After all, you were the one who started all that romantic business with the birthday cards and the flowery words."

She was hot! Anne convinced her to tone it down a bit. She read the next version to Debbie. Debbie suggested that she take it down a few more notches.

The following morning she dropped the watered-down version of her scathing letter in a mailbox on the way to church. She regretted it immediately.

Chapter 25

She had never written a letter like that before. Why did she do it? If only she could get it back. *It was a stupid thing to do,* she told herself on the way home from Mass. *You acted like a silly schoolgirl. What will Charles think? Maybe he really did have a problem in his family. What if he did intend to call her, and then he got her letter?*

She had ruined everything.

The rest of that day went by in a blur. When she got home from church, she cleaned the entire kitchen from top to bottom. Every wall, cabinet, drawer, and piece of woodwork got a thorough scrubbing whether it needed it or not. The curtains were taken down, washed, ironed, and put back up after the windows were washed. She exhausted herself until everything in her blue and white Dutch kitchen sparkled, and a scent of lemon detergent filled the air. She put Charles out of her mind in those hours, but later, after she went to bed, she found herself fretting about her letter again. She tossed restlessly all night long.

At ten thirty the next morning, her phone rang. She answered it half-heartedly.

"Rosemarie?"

Her heart stopped. Could it be Charles?

"Yes, who is this?"

"It's Charles. I just read your letter for the umpteenth time."

"Oh, Charles, I'm so sorry. I apologize. I shouldn't have sent it."

"Oh no. On the contrary. I'm so glad you did!"

"You are?"

"Yes, indeed! You know, after we talked that first time, I realized that you had no idea who I was. It broke my heart. I guess I was foolish, but the whole time I was sending you those birthday cards, I was hoping that between the shorthand and the other hints I gave, eventually you would remember me. When that didn't happen, I felt stupid and regretted telling you that I had fallen in love with you at Palmer. That's when I called and gave an excuse why we couldn't get together. I felt there wasn't any point in keeping in touch if you didn't know me.

"Then when I read your letter this morning, I could see that even though you didn't recall me, you were still interested. I read it over and over and got the feeling that you were disappointed that I didn't keep in touch." He chuckled. "Your words were a bit harsh in some places, but I guess I deserved it."

"Charles, I don't know what to say."

"Forget about it. Let's start all over again."

Chapter 26

"We were all wrong about why Charles didn't call," she said to Anne that evening. "He told me he was heartbroken after our first conversation. He was sure that I would remember him when we talked. When I didn't, he gave up on the idea of ever meeting me until he received my letter. I thought he would be annoyed with it, but he said it made him happy. He was pleased that even though I didn't know him, I was still interested enough to bawl him out for not staying in touch.

"Once we got over the letter business, we started to chat like we did in that first call. We discovered that we have a lot in common. He followed his sister into Palmer just like I did. Both of us like to read, and neither of us feels like eighty-seven. He even told me again that he had the hots for me when we were at Palmer. Can you imagine him saying that? I still can't believe that he went to so much trouble to find me. We talked for an hour."

"Did he make a date?" Anne asked when she took a breath.

"Not exactly. He said he would call me about getting together sometime soon. When I tried to pin him down, he asked when I was free. I told him Friday, next week."

"What did he say to that?"

"He said that he was going to visit his son next week and would call me when he got back. I think he really means it this time, Anne. I have a good feeling about it. I'm sure he'll call. How about coming up this weekend and taking me to the mall? I think I should have a new outfit, don't you? Just in case he makes a date."

On Friday, she went to her bowling banquet and came home with seventy-five dollars in prize money—fifty dollars for being on the second-place team and twenty-five dollars for the most improved bowler. The next day, Anne took her shopping to buy the perfect outfit for her to wear if or when Charles asked for a date.

Chapter 27

The shopping expedition was definitely an oddball, reverse, mother-daughter event. Rosemarie had to laugh that morning before Anne came when she realized how absurd it was that her fifty-five-year-old daughter was helping her, at age eighty-seven, to select clothes for a blind date. As ridiculous as that may be, it didn't change her ambition to look her best for Charles one bit.

She spent the entire afternoon with Anne, going through rack after rack of dresses, skirts, blouses, and pantsuits, trying many of them on before she was satisfied. By the time she made her selection, she was exuberant; Anne was exhausted. On the way home, Anne dubbed her "The Energizer Bunny."

Her battery finally ran down, though, as the weeks went by and Charles didn't call.

When Anne came for a visit in July, she was down in the dumps. All she wanted to do was talk about Charles.

"Why doesn't he call?"

"Charles might not be able to drive at his age," Anne suggested.

"Just because he is eighty-seven? I don't believe that! I know one woman who is ninety and still driving. Besides, he never mentioned that driving was a problem."

"It's a pretty long ride from Cape May to Haddonfield, Mother."

"OK, maybe he would need to stay overnight someplace. There's a nice bed-and-breakfast right off Kings Highway, only ten minutes from here. How about we take a ride and I'll pick up a brochure?"

Anne laughed. "You're not anxious to meet this guy, are you?"

"Let's just say I'm curious and want to be prepared if he calls."

"All right, let's go."

"Good." Rosemarie went to the closet, gathered her handbag, and asked on her way out the door, "Anne, after I get the brochure, can we stop at Shoe Town on Haddon Avenue? It's only a few blocks from there. I want a pair of white sandals to go with my new outfit—just in case."

She had not thrown in the towel yet.

Chapter 28

Two weeks later, sometime after nine, on a Wednesday evening, Rosemarie contacted Anne.

"Charles called tonight," she said breathlessly. "We have a lunch date at noon—a week from Friday. We decided to walk to the Jersey Diner around the corner so he wouldn't have to drive after he got here. He said he would leave for home around four."

Anne let out a whoop and encouraged her to tell her more.

"I told him I felt like a teenager going on a first date. He said he did, too. He said he could still remember how pretty I looked in the pink taffeta dress I wore to graduation. Isn't that something? He even remembered that I fell off the riser on the stage at rehearsal."

"Did you, really?"

"Yes. I was standing on the top row of the platform, and somehow it moved. Kathleen O'Brien and I both fell off. It was so embarrassing. It's hard to believe he remembers these things from so long ago. Anyway, I'm going to meet him, finally."

"I'd like to meet him too," Anne said too quickly. "Do you mind if I come up that day?"

"Why? Don't you think I can handle him by myself? Besides, you're working Friday."

"I'll ask for a day off. Look, I helped you get this far," Anne pleaded, "and I did talk to him, so I'm curious, too. I promise I won't intrude on your date. I'll go home when you leave for lunch."

"Well, I guess you deserve to be there. If you hadn't suggested that Matt and Kate try to find him, we wouldn't be having this date."

Though it was after ten o'clock when she ended her conversation with Anne, Rosemarie made herself a cup of coffee. She sat at the kitchen table thinking about Charles. It had been four years since he sent that first birthday card. In her wildest dreams she could never have imagined the story behind it or the man who sent it. *Ever since 1926 I have considered you my first love.* What was he thinking when he penned those words? She didn't even know he existed in 1926. Both had other loves and had lived a lifetime since then. Why did he send those cards? *Why did I send him that letter? Why do I want to meet him? It's all so crazy—so exciting, so outrageous at this time of my life.*

For the hundredth time she wondered what Charles looked like. His voice on the phone sounded deep and strong, bringing a tall, white-haired Clark Gable-type to mind, but she knew that was wishful thinking and not likely. What did it matter anyway? It's what a person is on the inside that matters most. That's what she taught her girls. Besides, Charles was definitely romantic. So what if he didn't look like Gable?

"I can't believe I'm going on a date!" She shivered and mused. "I wonder what Mike would think about all this."

Picturing her husband, the man she loved for most of her life, she talked to him in her mind as she did sometimes.

You don't mind, do you, Mike? There will never be anyone who could replace you in my heart, but I'm lonely, and this has been quite an adventure for me so far. I don't expect anything to come of it, but it is fun to think about dating again. This little fling probably won't last long, but it gives Charles and me something to think about besides dying. Please understand.

She knew he would. She turned out the kitchen light and went to bed.

Chapter 29

Charles drove to the AAA office in Cape May Court House the morning after his phone conversation with Rosemarie, singing his favorite old-time songs all the way. His deep voice floated out the open windows of his white Cadillac, entertaining anyone within earshot at every red light. Charles was oblivious—ecstatic with the thought of bringing his teenage fantasy to life.

Arriving at AAA in record time, he smiled at the pretty young blonde behind the counter and asked for a map of South Jersey and a street map of Haddonfield.

"Are you a triple-A member, sir?" the girl asked pleasantly.

"Oh yes, a longtime member," Charles replied, pulling his ID card from his wallet.

She checked his name and number and then turned to a long rack of maps behind her. Withdrawing the two he requested, she slid them into a clear plastic envelope and handed them to Charles, commenting, "I love Haddonfield. It is such a beautiful colonial town. Have you ever been there, Mr. Benson?"

"No. This is my first trip." He winked at her and said, "But I'm hoping it won't be my last."

Later, back home, he grabbed a handful of markers from his desk in the den and spread the maps on the kitchen table. He studied them carefully and then highlighted his route with a yellow marker.

An hour and a half easy, he thought. *To be on the safe side, I'll leave no later than nine.* He replaced the maps in their envelope and reached up to the calendar on the wall behind the table. With a black marker, he printed, "9:00 a.m. on Friday, July 14."

Whistling "Yankee Doodle Dandy," Charles carried the maps to his bedroom and laid them on his bureau. He opened the closet door beside the bureau and scanned the contents. His best suit—a brown pinstripe that he hardly ever wore—hung on a hook on the inside of the door in a blue plastic bag. It was fifteen years old. He figured it would do if he had it cleaned and pressed, but his shirts and ties were old and worn looking—not acceptable for a first date. He'd have to go shopping tomorrow and get new ones. Finally, he pulled a pair of dusty, brown leather shoes from the back of the closet. They had to shine on the fourteenth. He made a mental note to get his shoe-polishing kit up from the basement.

The following morning he called his barber.

"Joe, this is Charles Benson."

"Hey, Charles, haven't heard from you in a long time. How ya doin'?"

"I'm doing fine, Joe, but 1 need a haircut for something special. I have to look my best on Friday the fourteenth. When should I come in?"

"What's goin' on? You have a big date or somethin'?" Joe teased.

"As a matter of fact, I do!"

"You're kiddin'. Who'd wanna go out with an old coot like you?"

"An old girlfriend."

"Really? Well then, we better get you in for a trim. How 'bout you come in Tuesday at ten, lover boy? I wanna hear all about this girlfriend business."

"OK. It's a good story, Joe. You'll like this one."

Charles hung up the phone, drove to the cleaner's, dropped off his suit, and headed for Sears.

Every day from then on he did something to prepare for his date with Rosemarie, all the while trying to imagine what she looked like. Although he knew in his heart she would be different now, he envisioned her as he saw her last in Philadelphia—so beautiful—so shapely in her rose-colored suit, her dark hair falling in deep waves beneath her matching rose-colored hat. If only he could have spoken to her then...

Chapter 30

On the Saturday after Charles's call, Rosemarie walked to her beauty salon on Haddon Avenue for her weekly wash and set. Word of her annual anonymous birthday cards had made the rounds in the small shop over the last four years and was a favorite topic for the Saturday-morning regulars.

Rosemarie entered the shop all smiles.

As soon as she sat in Maureen's chair, she said, "You'll never guess what happened."

"What? You look like the cat that swallowed the canary, Rosemarie. Don't keep us in suspense. Is it something to do with your boyfriend?"

Ann Marie, the stylist working at the next chair, stopped talking to her seventy-something customer. Both were all ears.

"Yes, he called. I have a date next Friday!"

"Wow!" Maureen turned her head and spoke to the two women next to her. "Did you hear that, girls? Rosemarie has a date with her Romeo!"

Ann Marie begged, "Tell us all about it, Rosemarie."

"There's not much to tell except he's coming up from Cape May next Friday at noon, and we are going to the Jersey Diner for lunch."

"You are amazing," Ann Marie commented. "Having a date with a guy you don't even know at this time of your life. I'm jealous!"

Maureen spoke up. "Me too. This calls for a new hairstyle, don't you think?"

"Good idea," Rosemarie said. "And maybe a darker rinse?"

"Sure. We'll experiment this week, and if you like it, we'll have you looking like a new woman for your first date with your mystery man."

Rosemarie giggled. "Make me look younger, too."

"Of course! Would you like me to shape your eyebrows, too?"

"Why not?"

An hour later, Rosemarie made a big hit with her new look. Customers and stylists agreed she looked at least twenty years younger.

Elated, she told Maureen when she paid the bill, "Put me down for nine o'clock next Friday instead of Saturday, and I'd like an appointment Thursday afternoon for my nails. I might as well go all the way while I'm at it."

On the way to bowling Monday morning, she had a hard time not blurting out the story to her driver, Carol Wilson, but she kept the secret until her team sat down to put on their shoes.

"Girls, I have something to tell you." Rosemarie announced, loud enough for all to hear.

"What?" Carol asked, wondering why Rosemarie didn't tell her in the car.

With a little smile, she said mysteriously, "See if you can guess."

Carol jumped up from her seat. "Don't tell me you heard from Charles again."

"Yes, and he made a date for this Friday at noon!"

Four mature members of the Hot Shots team squealed in unison. Leaving shoes unlaced, they gathered around Rosemarie, bombarding her with questions.

"When did he call? What did he say? Where is he taking you? What are you going to wear?"

The first game was delayed fifteen minutes.

She was overwhelmed with the hullabaloo. Being the oldest bowler in the league, she occasionally created a stir with a high score, but today's news topped all previous honors. Even the male bowlers in the league were delighted to hear of her forthcoming date.

Tuesday, before Bible study began, everyone raved about her new hairstyle and color, but Rosemarie kept the reason for the change to herself until coffee. That was when she quietly mentioned to Joan O'Malley that she heard from Charles again, and that he made a date. Joan could not contain herself and immediately called for attention. "Girls! Girls! Rosemarie has a date with her mystery man!"

The group leader that week had no choice but to extend coffee for another twenty minutes while Rosemarie informed everyone about Charles's latest move. She felt like a teenager talking to girlfriends. They were all so excited for her.

On Thursday morning, she began to dust and vacuum the entire house. Every room had to be in tip-top shape. After all, this would be the first time Charles would meet her and see what kind of a housekeeper she was. Though this feature of date preparation might not be top on the list for many women, to her, it was important.

Why do you care? she asked herself. *You don't even know the man.*

She had no answer. It was just her way. As she worked, she imagined herself and Charles—whatever he looked like—walking around the corner to the Jersey Diner, talking and laughing like young people. The thought made her smile.

Chapter 31

The night before their date, Charles could not sleep. Uneasy thoughts crowded his mind. What if Rosemarie didn't like him? She was easy to talk to and seemed to like him over the telephone, but what would he do if they didn't click? What did she look like now? She was old like him, but she sounded younger. What if she was fat and not anything like the girl he remembered? What if their date was a disaster? Why did he start this whole thing?

But what if she *did* like him? What if they had a good time and wanted to see each other again? What if he could wine her and dine her, like he always dreamed of doing? What if he could really bring his fantasy alive? What then?

At midnight, Charles got up, went into the den, put a stack of records on the record player, and sat back in his comfortable La-Z-Boy to relax. The soothing voice of Bing Crosby crooning, "When You and I Were Seventeen," soon had him asleep and dreaming. *He was back at Palmer, sitting next to Rosemarie, holding her hand. She was talking and laughing with* him…

The scratching of the needle on the last record brought Charles back to consciousness in his home in Cape May. He got up quickly, turned off the machine, and returned to the bedroom. The clock on the night-stand read two o'clock.

A sliver of moonlight slipped under the shade onto the windowsill by the bed. Charles raised the shade all the way up, crept into bed, and with his arms behind his head, he stared out at the moon and thought of Rosemarie.

Chapter 32

On date day, Rosemarie hiked the mile to Saint Mary's Church, walking on air. She deliberately arrived early for the eight o'clock Mass to have a few quiet minutes to talk with God. Who else could she confide in only hours before meeting Charles for the first time?

Reaching her pew up front, Rosemarie placed her white leather handbag on the seat behind her and knelt to pray. "Dear God, I'm excited and nervous. What am I getting myself into? This man I'm going to meet in a few hours says he fell in love with me more than seventy years ago. I don't even know what he looks like, but he can tell me what I wore to graduation from Palmer. It's all so strange—his anonymous birthday cards, the way we found him. He sounds so nice. It isn't wrong for me to meet him, is it? I've been so lonely since Mike died. Charles makes me feel young again. He says such romantic things. I'm flattered that he remembers me after all this time. I am anxious to meet him. I hope he's a good man—someone I can trust. You must have put him in my life for some reason. Please help me through this day."

Leaving church, Rosemarie walked quickly to the beauty shop. As she took her seat, Maureen asked, "How are you doing this morning, Rosemarie? Nervous?"

"A little."

"A little! I'd be a wreck if it was me having the date. I can't imagine what I would say to a man I didn't even know."

"I don't think conversation will be a problem after we get over the shock of seeing each other." Rosemarie laughed. "I hope he doesn't think I look the same as I did the last time he saw me."

"You look pretty good for your age, and by the time I'm finished, you should look even younger. Are you OK with the color and style I gave you last week?"

"Absolutely! I've had compliments all week!"

Trying not to move her head as Maureen worked on her hair, she extended her right arm in front of her. "I'm so happy with my nails, too. I love the color!"

"I'm glad you like them. They should look great with your new outfit. This guy is really going to be impressed."

"I hope so. At least I made an effort to look my best."

"You'll be coming for your usual appointment next week, won't you?" Maureen asked. "You know the Saturday regulars will be dying to hear about your date."

Rosemarie smiled. "You can tell them all tomorrow that I'll be here unless my Prince Charming carries me away on his white charger!"

"Nothing that guy does would surprise me," Maureen commented.

An hour later, in her bedroom, Rosemarie removed her church clothes and slipped into a pink silk robe and slippers. She crossed the hall to the bathroom and, for the second time that morning, thoroughly washed and moisturized her face. Before the mirror, she carefully applied new liquid makeup, brown eyebrow pencil, rouge, and a little bit of "Pretty in Pink" lipstick. When she finished, she stood for a moment, admiring this younger-looking lady with the stylish brown hair who looked back at her. This woman looked more like the person she felt she was than the wrinkled old lady who usually appeared. That made her happy.

Humming, she returned to her bedroom and took her new pink and white flowered two-piece outfit from the closet and laid it on the bed. The new white sandals were placed with her white straw handbag on the love seat in front of the window. Perfume and jewelry were arranged on the top of her bureau. Rosemarie savored every remaining moment in the female predate ritual of primping. Primping for a man she did not know.

Chapter 33

$\mathcal{B}$y six thirty on the morning of Friday, July 14, Charles was up. He showered, shaved, and dressed in his blue flannel bathrobe and brown corduroy slippers. He shuffled down the hall to the kitchen. Mechanically, he filled a one-cup coffeepot sitting on the counter near the sink with water from the tap and a tablespoon of coffee from the can in the refrigerator. Plugging the pot into the outlet behind the kitchen table, he moved on his usual morning circuit, gathering cornflakes from the pantry, a bowl from the cabinet, and his mug from the dish drainer on the counter. He put them all on a faded, flowered placemat, where he usually sat at the table, and then realized he wasn't hungry. The prospect of meeting Rosemarie in just a few hours had him jittery.

He turned on the radio and listened to the news as he paced the kitchen floor, waiting for the coffee. From the window at the sink, he caught a glimpse of his "pride and joy" in the driveway. His newly cleaned and polished white 1980 Cadillac (with the red leather seats that he loved) sparkled like a gem in the early-morning sunlight. He grinned boyishly.

Feeling confident now and more at ease, he sauntered back to his bedroom to get the maps. His eyes scanned the room. Everything was in order. His bed was made. His brown suit—fresh from the cleaners—hung from the top of the closet door. Below it on the doorknob, his new white shirt hung, pressed with a new tie around the neck. His polished brown shoes lay beneath an old maple chair beside the bed, with brown socks inside. His wallet filled with cash lay on the bureau near the maps, along with a small bottle of breath spray and his car keys.

He grabbed the bag with the maps and returned to the kitchen table to study them one last time with his coffee. He had gone over them so many times that he felt he could drive to Haddonfield in his sleep.

At nine o'clock Charles stood in the driveway next to his sparkling white chariot—keys in hand, dressed to the nines, pocket full of money, heart full of hope.

Chapter 34

Rosemarie expected Charles at noon. She was completely dressed, nervous, and excited when Anne arrived at eleven. She offered her a cup of tea, but Anne refused. She couldn't take a thing. She was on edge, too. They chose to sit opposite each other at either end of the living room. Rosemarie—in her mahogany rocking chair—faced the door, tapping her foot. Anne sat near the fireplace in a straight-back chair, trying to be inconspicuous. For the first twenty minutes they chatted about everything and anything but Charles. They then fell silent, each lost in her own thoughts.

Rosemarie stared at the door, wondering if Charles would show up. She didn't know what to expect. Would he back out at the last minute? She felt a twinge in the pit of her stomach. What did he look like? What would he say when he saw her? Would he be shocked at her appearance, or pleased with her new look? Suppose she didn't like him? What would she do? To add to her unease, her two brothers—both in their eighties themselves—recently expressed concern that this unknown Romeo might be some kind of a crackpot. They were worried for her safety and thought she was too trusting.

She had no idea that Anne was worrying about her date, too. Anne was recalling the numerous discussions she'd had with Debbie over the past week about their mother's first date with the mystery man. Up to this point, they had both enjoyed the romantic adventure tremendously—the anonymous birthday cards, finding the Phantom Romeo, and hearing his story. It had all unfolded like a fairy tale. Page by page they were totally enchanted with it. But now Prince Charming was stepping off the page, out of the book, and into reality. They weren't sure if they were ready for that. Once the date loomed before them, there were lots of questions. What kind of a man was this Charles Benson? What was he thinking about when he asked their mother for a date? Did Charles possibly have the illusion of seventeen-year-old Rosemarie in his mind when he made this date? How would he react when he saw the eighty-seven-year-old woman she had become? Would he be the gentleman they imagined?

Suddenly, shrill sounds erupted simultaneously amid the angst-filled silence in the room. Both women shuddered as the mantel clock bonged the first of twelve times, and the doorbell chimed noisily at the front door.

It was noon. Charles was here!

Chapter 35

*R*osemarie, heart pumping, rose from her chair. The lines on her forehead softened. She took a deep breath, walked to the door, and opened it slowly.

There stood her Romeo—a slightly built, elderly man with a twinkle in his blue eyes and a cane in his right hand.

Smiling at him, she asked timidly, "Charles?"

"Yes, it's me. Finally," he said, with a little laugh. "After all this time."

A bespectacled man, bald but for a fringe of white hair, stepped into the living room. Clad nattily in a brown, pinstriped suit, white shirt, and brown striped tie, he carefully leaned his wooden cane against the wall next to the door. Turning to Rosemarie, he took both of her hands in his. Much to her surprise, he drew her to him and gently kissed her cheek. Then holding her away from himself, he took a long look and smiled as if he were gazing once again at the lovely young girl from his youth.

"You are still beautiful, Rosemarie."

With heart thumping wildly, Rosemarie could feel her face burning. Caught off guard, she was stunned. Finally, she regained her composure enough to smile. She made some nonsensical remark and led Charles to the love seat, where she sat down beside him.

Anne stayed at the back of the room, not saying a word or moving a muscle, as she witnessed Charles's fantasy coming to life.

Rosemarie asked Charles about his trip to Haddonfield. Did he have any trouble finding the house? How long did it take him to drive here?

Her questions and his answers flowed easily between them and then, suddenly, she remembered that Anne was there.

"Oh, Charles, I'm sorry! There is someone I want you to meet."

Motioning Anne to come to the love seat, she said, "Charles, this is Anne—the daughter who found you."

He chuckled and said, "Hi. I guess you're the one I talked to on the phone."

"Yes, that was me."

Charles and Anne chatted back and forth, recalling their long conversation months ago.

After a few minutes, Rosemarie stood up. Looking directly at Anne, she said, "Excuse us, Anne, it's time we leave for lunch."

Then looking back at Charles, she said, "Charles, you must be starved after that long ride."

He smiled and nodded.

Taking the hint, Anne said, "Sure, I have to go anyway."

Stepping away from them, she returned to the other end of the room for her handbag, kissed her mother on the way out the door, and said to Charles, "It was nice to meet you, Mr. Benson. Enjoy your lunch."

Struggling to get up from the love seat, Charles answered, "Nice to meet you, too, Anne. I'm sure Rosemarie and I will have a good lunch." Winking at her, he said, "It will probably last all afternoon. We have a lot of catching up to do."

Ten minutes later, Rosemarie and Charles walked arm in arm down the front steps and up the street on the way to the Jersey Diner, like young people out on a date. Left behind by the front door was the brown, wooden cane—no longer needed as Charles and the girl in his dreams stepped back to their youth.

Part 2
The Romance

Chapter 36

Charles drove away from Haddonfield in his shining white Cadillac at four thirty.

On the way home, he had a lot to think about but tried hard to keep his mind on the road. He didn't want to repeat the mishap he'd had on the way up. He blamed it on lack of sleep, but nevertheless, he had dozed off at the wheel momentarily on the way to Haddonfield. Fortunately, it was on a deserted part of the journey, and lucky for him, he woke up when the front wheel hit the curb and not a telephone pole.

He wouldn't have told Rosemarie about it at all, except that he sensed her disappointment when he didn't mention seeing her again at the restaurant. He definitely wanted their relationship to continue, but he realized that driving that far again would be dangerous. After the good time they had today, he had to let her know why he didn't make another date.

As he drove, his last half hour with Rosemarie played back in his mind.

On their walk back to her house after lunch, he began slowly. "I had a little problem on the way up here, Rosemarie." Then he told her the rest in as few words as possible.

She stopped walking and turned to him with a worried look on her face and said, "Charles, you could have been hurt. Do you think it's safe for you to drive back? There's a bed-and-breakfast not far from here. You could stay there overnight and leave in the morning. I have some information on it at the house if you want to see it."

He was pleased with her concern and very amused by her suggestion that he stay at a bed-and-breakfast instead of her house. Patting her hand, he assured her, "Don't get upset, dear. I feel fine after our wonderful visit. To be on the safe side, though, I think I better find another way of seeing you from now on."

When they reached the house, she invited him in. As they sat on the love seat by the front door, he took her hand and said, "Rosemarie, I'd like to see you again, but until I figure out how I can do it without driving, do you think we could have a phone date once a week?"

"I'd like that," she answered.

"Great! Do you have anything on your schedule for Wednesday evenings?"

"No, Wednesdays are good," she replied.

He hugged her. "Then that's what we'll do. I'll call you every Wednesday at seven. Somehow we have to keep this thing going now that we finally had our first date."

"I'll look forward to that, but will you call tonight after eight thirty so I know you got home safely?"

"Sure, but why do I have to wait until eight thirty?"

"I'm working at the rectory for a few hours tonight answering the phone."

He grinned. Rosemarie was certainly a busy woman.

Although he wanted so much to kiss her good-bye on the lips, he did not. After this perfect day, he didn't want to do anything to jeopardize Rosemarie's first impression of him. He retrieved his cane from the wall by the door and left her with another hug and a kiss on the cheek.

Chapter 37

The phone was ringing when Rosemarie returned from the rectory that evening. Rushing to her desk in the dining room, she picked up the receiver.

"Charles?"

"No. It's me—Anne. I couldn't wait any longer. Tell me about your date."

"I just got in this minute from the rectory. I was expecting Charles to call."

"Wow! That must have been some date if you two have to talk again tonight," Anne teased.

"Oh, for heaven's sake—I just wanted to make sure he got home all right."

"OK, so tell me about your date."

"Don't get so excited. It was just a lunch."

"Come on, it must have been more interesting than that!"

"OK, OK. We walked around the corner to the diner, as you know. When we went in, Millie, the hostess, recognized me. I go there for breakfast sometimes with my church friends. Millie asked where we would like to sit."

Her voice became more animated as she continued. "Before I could say a word, Charles spoke up and said we would like a booth in the corner. After we ordered, Charles took my hand. I was so embarrassed and afraid that one of the waitresses would notice, but he didn't care. He told me how happy he was to finally have a date with me after all this time. He repeated most of what he said in our first conversation about him falling in love with me at Palmer and how disappointed he was when he lost track of me. Then he squeezed my hand and said, 'I'm so glad I found you at last.'

"Isn't he something? We talked for hours. He told me all about his family and his life these last seventy years, and I did the same. We had a lovely time. I guess our waitress was wondering what was going on. We didn't leave until after three thirty."

"Well, what do you think of him?" Anne asked.

"He's very nice, and such a gentleman, but..." she said and then stopped.

"But what?"

"Well," she laughed and said in a voice Anne could barely hear, "he looks older than me."

"But he's the same age."

Rosemarie sighed. "I know, I know, but I don't feel that old."

"That's because you never act your age, Mother!" Anne said, laughing.

She laughed, too. She had to admit that she took great pride in the fact that unlike most people her age, she deliberately kept herself busy and physically fit, secretly believing that she was holding age ninety at bay. In her mind, Charles, the pleasant man who arrived with a cane for their first date, couldn't possibly be her age.

"Well, make up your mind. Do you like him or not?" Anne asked.

"Yes, I do like him. We had a good time. By the way, he doesn't act his age either."

When the call ended, Rosemarie sat for a long time pondering the events of the day. She was amazed with it all. Was this really happening? Like magic, Charles had erased seventy years. She giggled as she pictured herself a modern-day Alice in Wonderland, stepping out of old age and into Charles's fantasy as a seventeen-year-old once again.

Chapter 38

Promptly at seven the following Wednesday evening, Charles called.

On the second ring, she answered.

"Hello, Rosemarie. How are you doing?"

"Oh, I'm fine, Charles. How are you?"

"Missing you very much and anxious to see you again."

"I'd like to see you, too. I really enjoyed our date."

"I'm trying to cook up some way for us to get together," Charles said, "but so far, I haven't had any luck. I'll keep working on it, though. You can be sure about that. You think about it, too. Maybe between the two of us we'll come up with something."

Their conversation continued for more than an hour as they went back in time, recalling events and places from their younger days in Philadelphia.

"Do you remember when the Delaware River Bridge opened in 1926?" Charles asked.

"Sure, I remember," Rosemarie said. "My girlfriends and I walked all the way from the Philadelphia side to the Jersey side and back. Thousands of people were there. It was like a big party as people from Jersey walked past us going the other way. It was so exciting!"

Charles told a story about a huge warehouse fire five blocks from his home when he was a boy. "My sister and I watched teams of horses racing through our neighborhood pulling the fire wagons," he said. "We could see the flames rising over the row houses high in the sky from our bedroom windows."

With the mention of horses, Rosemarie told Charles how much she loved them.

"I especially admired the horses the police rode in the city," she commented. "They were huge, handsome animals and so well kept. After I started working, I took riding lessons at a stable in Fairmount Park."

"Somehow, I can't picture you riding a horse," Charles said, chuckling.

"Well, I did! In fact, I rode almost every Saturday morning for years."

Down memory lane, they went recalling the sounds of the yellow, metal trolley cars they took to Palmer, screeching to a stop on the metal tracks on Market Street as showers of sparks came up from the tracks and down from the cables above.

They talked about the music of Paul Whitman, songs by Bing Crosby, the flight of Charles Lindbergh, and the Depression—all topics they experienced but hadn't talked about for years. Their reminiscing invigorated both of them and made them yearn for more.

"I'll call you next Wednesday at seven," Charles said as they ended the call that evening.

"I'll look forward to that," Rosemarie replied. "It's so good talking with someone who shares your memories."

"I agree," Charles replied. "I feel so lucky that I persisted in finding you, Rosemarie. You are everything I dreamed you would be. What a dummy I was not to ask you for a date at Palmer!"

Chapter 39

"$\mathscr{I}$'m going to Ocean City for a vacation with Anne's family in September," Rosemarie said to Charles, several weeks later. "How far is that from Cape May?"

"Oh, it's not far—maybe about an hour. Why?"

"I was thinking about asking Anne to drive me over to Cape May while we are down that way so we could have a little visit."

"Great idea!"

"I'm not sure it will work, though. I didn't realize you would be an hour away. That might be too much to ask."

"Wait a minute. Don't give up so fast. Let's talk about it. We can't pass up an opportunity like this. If Anne could drop you off at the mall in the center of Cape May for the afternoon, I can handle everything from there."

"That sounds good, but I wouldn't feel right asking her to give up that much time with her family. She was looking forward to this time with her son, Matt; and his wife, Kate; and their son, Bryan. I was, too. Bryan is my first great-grandchild. They live so far away from us that we rarely get to see them. That's why this vacation in Ocean City is so important to all of us. If I ask Anne to take me to Cape May, it would take most of one day by the time she takes me there, drives back to Ocean City, and then makes the return trip. No, I don't think that will work."

"Hold on! How about if Kate and Bryan come to Cape May with you?" Charles asked. "There's a nice zoo not far from the mall where they could go for the afternoon while we have our date. It's free, too. What do you think?"

"That's perfect! I didn't mention any of this to Anne yet, but I'm sure she and Kate will go for it. As far as I know, they've never been to that zoo. Charles, you have the best ideas!"

"Thank you, my dear, but let's give credit to where it is due. You came up with the suggestion in the first place. Don't waste any time contacting Anne, because once I get the go-ahead, I'll plan a day you won't forget."

Chapter 40

"Why doesn't he just drive over to see you in Ocean City?" Anne asked after Rosemarie presented her "Cape May Visit with Charles" idea the next evening on the phone.

Carefully choosing her words, Rosemarie began, "Well, Charles had a little problem on the way up to my house last month, so we both agreed he shouldn't drive much anymore. That's why I wondered if you could take me over to see him while we're at the shore, if it's not too much trouble. He said Cape May is about an hour's drive from Ocean City, and we could meet him near the fountain in the outdoor mall. He suggested we bring Kate and Bryan along and the three of you could go to the Cape May Zoo while we have our visit."

"What was Charles's *little problem*, Mother?" Anne asked.

"Nothing to worry about. Do you think you could take me to see him?"

"Did he have an accident?" Anne persisted.

"It was just a little one. If you must know, he fell asleep at the wheel and drove off the road. Probably because it was such a long ride." Hearing a gasp at the other end of the line, she added quickly, "He didn't hurt himself or anyone else. He only dozed off for a second. Now tell me if you can take me to see him so we can make some plans."

After her explanation, Anne agreed to the proposed trip to Cape May in September, but this incident made her realize that this fun romance between her mother and Charles—one that she encouraged up until now—was getting complicated.

Three weeks later, around ten thirty on a Wednesday morning, an entourage of Rosemarie, Anne, Kate, and Bryan piled into Anne's car for the ride to Cape May.

The night before, Anne had asked if she and Charles had any definite plans for the next day. She told her that Charles wanted to surprise her.

On the way to Cape May, Rosemarie read over the list of restaurants and shops in the Cape May mall that Anne had given her the night before they left.

"It would be best to stay in the mall, Mother," Anne cautioned. "Charles uses a cane and probably can't walk too far."

"Thanks for the information. I'll show it to Charles," she said, but she had no intention of doing so.

Her daughter meant well, but Rosemarie already knew some of Charles's plans for the day. Anne wouldn't like them. She smiled to herself.

The hour ride down the parkway was a real treat. She was happy to be with the girls and Bryan even though she had to put up with teasing about her date.

Kate kidded, "Charles will probably take you to McDonald's for lunch, Grandmom. I bet he orders a Big Mac special with French fries for the both of you."

"Oh, come on, Kate," she said with her nose scrunched up. "He wouldn't dare!"

"I agree with you, Mother," Anne chimed in. "He would never take you to McDonald's. My guess is that he'll treat you to a beer and a pizza at the Ugly Mug in the mall."

She groaned. "That's worse!"

They all laughed.

It was a gorgeous sunny day with temperatures in the eighties. There was not a cloud in the sky. Bryan, from his car seat near the window in the backseat, was excited and babbling as he watched the seagulls coasting overhead. Everyone was in a good mood. The day couldn't have been nicer.

She was hoping Charles would like her new pink, striped, seersucker dress with three-quarter sleeves and notice the lily-of-the-valley perfume she dabbed behind her ears. She felt happy, humming a little tune when the joking ceased.

As they approached Cape May, Kate commented, "You look great in pink, Grandmom. I bet you'll knock his socks off."

"You really do look lovely, Mother," Anne agreed.

She blushed. "Thanks, girls. Better watch out. You'll give me a big head."

As the mall came into view, Rosemarie was excited, like a fifteen-year-old who told one thing to her parents and did something else.

Chapter 41

At eleven thirty, Charles found a seat on a bench near the fountain in the Cape May mall. The place was crowded with seniors enjoying a perfect day at the shore. He reached into his shirt pocket and, feeling safe that no one would notice, withdrew a small bottle of breath spray and gave himself a few quick shots. Everything had to be perfect today. Early that morning, before his shower, he followed the exercise routine Rosemarie had suggested on one of their first phone dates—ten minutes of marching and twenty minutes on his stationary bike. He couldn't do that much when he started a month ago, but now he could follow the regime exactly. Rosemarie was right—he did feel stronger and no longer needed his cane. Rosemarie was good for him. For her, he carefully pressed his yellow, short-sleeved shirt and navy slacks last night. For her, he wore a new, white, baseball cap to hide his bald head. For her, he planned a day to remember.

He watched the crowd closely. At eleven forty-five, he caught sight of Rosemarie and her family approaching the mall from the parking lot across the street. Rosemarie saw him almost at the same instant. She left her family and hurried to him. He stood up, gave her a hug and a kiss, and then as the rest of the family reached him, he greeted them with hugs and kisses, too—like family.

Kate took photographs of the two of them at the ornate Cape May sign in front of the fountain. Then some kind bystander—thinking that they were a family of four generations—offered to take a photo of them all. Charles grinned, happy that the event was recorded for posterity.

Soon after, he gave Anne directions to the zoo, recommending that she leave immediately before more seniors arrived by bus.

"We'll meet back here at four," he said. "Have a good time."

"You too," Anne said.

With a big smile on his face, Charles replied, "Oh, we will for sure." As they parted ways, he reached for Rosemarie's hand. Smugly, they sauntered down the mall, stopping to look in store windows every now and then, as innocent as could be, supposedly following Anne's suggestions.

Chapter 42

*H*ours later, Anne, Kate, and Bryan arrived back at the mall well before the appointed time. Bryan was sound asleep in his stroller. Kate and Anne, exhausted by their never-ending hike around the huge Cape May Zoo, collapsed on a long bench near the fountain. At four o'clock, Charles and Rosemarie, arm in arm, meandered down the mall toward them. As they came closer, the girls could see that he was beaming; she was flushed. There was no doubt they had enjoyed their day.

"Could we sit for a few minutes before we leave, Anne?" Rosemarie asked.

"Sure," Anne replied as she made room for them on the bench.

"We had a wonderful day," Rosemarie began. "Charles took me to the lighthouse first. We didn't go up to the top, but we walked all around the bottom and visited the information center. It was so interesting! I've never seen a lighthouse before. Have either of you?"

"Yes, I toured this one a few years ago," Anne said, worry lines forming on her forehead. No question about it, Charles had driven there.

Rosemarie didn't wait for Kate to answer but went right on, "After that, Charles gave me a tour of the whole town. There are so many antique shops and such beautiful Victorian homes. There was so much to see."

Charles sat close to her, smiling as she rambled on. "We went to a gorgeous restaurant on the beach for lunch and sat by a window, where we could see the ocean. It was just marvelous! After lunch we drove to Sunset Beach, where they have the cutest little shops."

At this point Anne interrupted, "Well, it sounds like you two had quite a day, and you don't look half as tired as Kate and I feel. I think we better get on the road. It'll be an hour before we get home." They all stood up. Anne said to Charles, "Good to see you again, Charles."

"Nice to see you, too." He gave her a hug, saying, "Thanks so much, Anne, for making this day possible for Rosemarie and me. We truly enjoyed it."

Kate extended her hand, smiled, and said, "Nice to meet you, Mr. Benson."

"I'm happy to meet you too, Kate. If it's not too much trouble, I'd like a copy of those pictures you took today."

"Sure. When I get them developed, I'll give them to Grandmom."

"Thanks so much." Nodding at Bryan asleep in his stroller, Charles remarked, "That's a handsome little fella you have there. I can see why Rosemarie thinks so much of him."

Kate smiled.

Turning to Rosemarie he gave her a kiss on the cheek and whispered, "I'll call you next Wednesday."

On the ride back to Ocean City, Rosemarie filled in the missing details of her date.

"He wanted to buy me some jewelry, but I refused. I told him he had already spent too much money on me with the fabulous lunch and fancy French wine."

Anne's face blanched at the mention of wine.

"I told him he was spoiling me. He laughed and said he had to make up for lost time. And then…"

After a half hour, Rosemarie stopped talking. For the rest of the trip back to Ocean City, she remained quiet, gazing out of the car window – a Mona Lisa smile on her lips.

Chapter 43

*C*harles woke up happy as a lark the next morning. Memories of his day with *the girl in his dreams* drifted through his mind as he showered and lingered long after breakfast was over. His favorite recollection was the lunch they had at "Tallulah's By the Sea." He thought Rosemarie would like that place. She raved about the spectacular view of the ocean from their table, and once the French wine was poured, the two of them talked and laughed like the young couples seated near them. There was only one disappointment. She wouldn't let him buy her a piece of jewelry as a remembrance of their day together. He had planned that to be the perfect ending of their date, but she wouldn't hear of it.

He recalled her words as they sat on a bench in front of the jewelry store in the mall. *"It's so nice of you to think of doing something like that, Charles, but I couldn't accept it. You've already spent too much money on me. You're spoiling me!"* Smiling sweetly, she said, *"You can be sure I'll remember this day, Charles, and without a souvenir. It was just wonderful! Thank you so much."*

Eyes closed, he pictured her in her pink and white striped dress, remembering the scent of her floral perfume. He wanted so much to see her again. He had to tell her what the day meant to him.

He quickly walked to the den and found a pen and some writing paper in his desk and returned to the kitchen table. Twenty minutes later, letter in hand, he whistled all the way to the mailbox three blocks away. *Rosemarie would be happy to see me walking. More exercise to keep me healthy.*

Chapter 44

*R*osemarie, on cloud nine for the rest of her vacation in Ocean City, rose to cloud ten when she arrived back home to find a letter from Charles in her mailbox.

Thursday, Sept. 10, 1996

Dear Rosemarie,
Welcome Home! I miss you already!!!!!

Hope you had a great vacation with your family in Ocean City. I was happy to meet Anne's daughter-in-law Kate, and Bryan-your first great-grandson!

I enjoyed our day together yesterday tremendously and hope you felt the same. I'll try to figure a way for us to have more dates like that in the future. Would you like that?

Time for lunch, so I will sign off for now and get this out to the mailbox to be certain it will arrive by the time you get back home. Take care, my dear. I'll call you on Wednesday.

Charles

Chapter 45

Weeks went by with the Wednesday-night phone calls fanning the flames of their romance. Then one Wednesday, in late October, Rosemarie's phone was silent at seven. She busied herself for a while folding laundry, but after an hour she started getting nervous. At eight o'clock, just as she was about to call Charles, the phone rang. She picked it up immediately.

"Charles?"

"No. I'm Charles's grandson, Bill," a man said. "Is this Rosemarie?"

Rosemarie's stomach churned. "Yes, I'm Rosemarie. Is Charles all right?"

"He's OK now, but he had a little heart trouble yesterday. He's in Ocean View Hospital in Cape May. When I visited him tonight, he told me about your Wednesday-night phone dates. He asked if I would let you know why he didn't call."

"Thanks, Bill, I do appreciate your call so much. Is there anything I can do for him?"

"Well, he's going to be in the hospital for a few days for observation, and he was wondering if you could come down to see him. I hate to even mention it because I know you live quite a ways from here, but I promised I would ask."

"I don't drive, Bill, but I'll see if I can get someone to bring me down tomorrow. Does he have a phone in his room?"

"No, but you can pass a message through the floor nurse if you want to. He's on the second floor, room 233."

"I'll do that as soon as I get a ride," Rosemarie said. "Thanks, again, for calling."

"Oh, you're welcome. I know Pop Pop thinks a lot of you, Rosemarie. He'll be real happy if you can make it down."

"I'll try my best."

After she hung up from Bill, Rosemarie thought about her relationship with Charles. She liked being special to someone again and enjoyed the attention from this man. The dates, notes, and phone calls made her feel young again. Now what? Had her romantic bubble burst? Was their age finally catching up to them? She wasn't ready to face reality. She cried. An hour later she called Anne.

"I'm sorry to phone you at this hour, but I just found out that Charles is in the hospital. I have to talk to somebody."

"What happened?"

"His grandson, Bill, called me tonight. Charles had heart trouble yesterday and was taken to a hospital in Cape May. The doctors aren't sure what's going on, so they want to keep him under observation for a few days. Charles asked Bill to contact me. He wants me to come down. I'm worried. Is there any way you could get off from work tomorrow and take me to see him?"

"It's too late for me to call my boss now, Mother," Anne said, "but I'll go in early tomorrow and tell them I need the afternoon off for personal reasons. I'll pick you up at one. That should get us to the hospital by two thirty. You can stay all afternoon if you like."

Chapter 46

"I'm calling about patient Charles Benson in room 233," Rosemarie said to the nurse on the second floor the following morning.

"Yes, what can I do for you?"

"Would you please tell Mr. Benson that Rosemarie will be down to visit him this afternoon somewhere around two thirty? He's waiting to hear from me."

"I'll be glad to. He seems down in the dumps today. He could use a pick-me-up. I'll give him your message right away."

Rosemarie arrived at the hospital anxious and on edge. Anne saw her to Charles's room on the second floor and then excused herself, saying she would be in the lounge at the end of the hall.

When Rosemarie entered his room, Charles was sitting up in bed, in a hospital gown, looking pale but well groomed. His face broke into a huge smile as soon as he caught sight of her.

"Am I ever glad to see you!"

Rosemarie, her brow furrowed, hurried to the bedside and grasped Charles's hand. "How are you, Charles? I've been so worried."

"I'm much better now that I can see you."

The lines on Rosemarie's face softened, and her cheeks reddened as she smiled.

"Sit down, dear," Charles said as he motioned her to a chair next to the bed.

"I'm so glad you could come. I've missed you so much, especially these last two days. Our phone dates are nice, but seeing you in person is the best."

"I've missed you, too, but you didn't have to go to all this trouble to see me."

"Believe me, this wasn't my idea. This body of mine has its own ideas sometimes. Really aggravates me."

"What happened?"

"Well, I was having a good time on Tuesday afternoon, playing cards with my friends at the VFW, when all of a sudden I felt like I was going to pass out. The next thing I knew, two young fellas were loading me into an ambulance. By the time I got to the hospital, I felt better and wanted to go home, but the doctors wouldn't go for it. They insisted on a million tests and told me I had to stay here for a few days to see what's going on. My grandson, Bill, lives the closest, so they called him, and he came down. All that fuss for nothing. I feel fine, but at least I got to see you again."

"Did they give you any idea why you passed out?"

"So far, they think it has something to do with my circulation. Maybe I was sitting down too long. I don't know. I didn't have anything to drink, so that wasn't it, but they're still doing tests. I feel good, so I think they're just giving me a once-over. Hopefully, I'll be home tomorrow. Don't worry. With all this time on my hands, I'm getting some good ideas for our next date."

"Oh, for heaven's sake, Charles—you have to get out of here first."

"I'll be all right. Bill and I have had a good chance to talk while I'm stuck in here, and we're working something out. When it's all set, I'll let you know. In the meantime, I have a little surprise for you. Open your hand."

Charles reached under the covers. He brought out a small white box with a tiny pink rose on top and placed it in her hand.

Flabbergasted, Rosemarie asked, "What's this, Charles? You're the patient. I should have brought you something."

"Never mind that," Charles said, his face wreathed in smiles. "Open it."

"The package is so pretty I hate to ruin it." Carefully she removed the rose, sat it on the bed, and opened the lid.

"Oh, how beautiful!" she exclaimed as she gazed at a pair of silver pierced earrings shaped like seashells, each with a tiny diamond in the center. "Charles, you shouldn't have! What's this all about? Where did you get these?"

"I asked Bill to get them for me this morning. He went back to the mall—to that little jewelry shop I wanted to take you to in September. This is what I wanted to buy for you that day, but you wouldn't let me. I want you to have them, Rosemarie. Now enjoy them!"

Tears in her eyes, Rosemarie leaned over and kissed Charles.

"I don't know what to say. They are lovely. Thank you."

As she came close to him, Charles noticed that Rosemarie wore clip earrings.

Disappointed, he said, "Uh oh, looks like there's a problem. You don't have pierced ears. I'll have Bill exchange them."

"You'll do no such thing. I love them. I'll take care of it. I've never had a reason to get my ears pierced before, but I do now!"

The following morning Rosemarie—a bit nervous over what she was about to do—rode the senior bus to the Cherry Hill mall for her first visit to the Piercing Pagoda.

Chapter 47

*D*uring his recovery, Charles continued the Wednesday-night phone dates but decided to enhance his wooing a bit by sending Rosemarie cards and letters from time to time. Somewhere in most missives he wrote a secret endearment in shorthand.

Nov. 19, 1997

My Dear Rosemarie,
It was wonderful to hear your cheery voice yesterday. I was "blue and down in the dumps," so I thought I would call. You sounded so happy to hear from me.

After we talked I felt as though the sun came out of the clouds and everything was bright and pleasant once again. See what effect you have on me?

Right after Thanksgiving, I'll be flying to Austin, Texas, for a few weeks to visit with my daughter Pat and her husband. When I come back on December 20, Chuck, my son, will pick me up at the airport, and I'll be with him in Quakertown, Pennsylvania, until after Christmas. How long? Who knows?

Ever since I had that little problem in October, everybody is concerned about me staying by myself. I keep telling them that I'm OK. I feel fine, but nobody listens to me. I guess I should be thankful that they care about me.

Anyway, when I get situated, I'll write and give you their addresses. Please write back. I'll be looking forward to getting letters from you.

⌇ [In his shorthand, he added *and always will.*]

Your devoted,
Charles

Dec. 5, 1997

2019 Furlong Drive
Austin, Texas 32974

Dear Rosemarie,
I received your very nice letter. You write just the way you talk, and that pleases me very much. I miss you and will be glad to get back north to be closer to you.
    Don't forget ⌇ [Added in his shorthand: *very much, hour after hour.*]
    So long my beautiful one. I'll be seeing you in my dreams.
Charles

Dec. 15, 1997

My Darling Rosemarie,
I'm not too clever with pen and ink,
At writing down all the things I think,
But this comes to say what's certainly true-
There's hardly a day when I don't think of you.
<u>Never!</u>
⌇

Charles

Dec. 22, 1997

66 Deerfield Pike
Quakertown, PA 23479

My Dear Rosemarie,
I miss you so much.

I cannot get out to a store to buy you a nice Christmas card, Sweetheart, but I want to wish you a grand and Merry Christmas. Hoping we both have a great and wonderful 1998.

Chuck and Ann will be taking me home to Cape May on Saturday, January 10. He said we could stop to see you on the way down, but he wants to get an early start. I suggested that I treat you all to breakfast at the same place where we had our first date. What do you think, Sweetheart? You'll be back from Mass by nine thirty, won't you? This will be a good chance for you to meet some of my family. Hope you are free that day.

So long, my beautiful one. Hope to see you soon. Don't forget, [in his shorthand he adds] *I'll love you forever.* Hope you can still read this old Benn-Pitman shorthand!

Luv U,
Charles

Jan. 6, 1998

My Darling Rosemarie,
Happy New Year! Received your very pleasant letter. I'm so happy that you are free on Saturday. We'll be at your house at 9:30am. I can't wait to see you—even though we'll have company.

You say my birthday card to you sounded like it came from a much younger fella. Since we are both now 88, how about adding the two 8s, making us exactly 16.

107

I went to the doctor this morning, and he gave me some good news. My heartbeat is OK-despite my having finally gotten together with you! Anyhow, it appears that I am going to keep going a little bit longer.

It will be so good to get home and back to our Wednesday-night phone dates. I do enjoy our correspondence very much, but I miss hearing your voice. How about we do both from now on?

Charles

Don't forget 8 + 8 is 16. Try to remember that and act accordingly!

PS The stamps on the envelope were positioned upside down purposely. Glad you knew why!

Jan. 16, 1998

Dearest Rosemarie,

Was just reading your last letter for the umpteenth time. I'm glad that you enjoyed the visit with my son and his wife. It was so good to see you again. You looked beautiful as always and I was so happy to see that you wore the ear-rings I gave you in October. It's been a long three months! I'll have to figure some way for us to get together again soon.

It's so good to be home. I'm trying to follow your advice on keeping fit. You said to exercise on my bike, so I did today even tho' it was 29 degrees on my enclosed but <u>unheated</u> porch. I swear my bike said "thank you, sir" when I left!

The shorthand "Logo" in my last letter seems to have you puzzled. How about this shorthand: *I love you, believe that I love you, with all of my heart.*

Now can you read it? Or has it been too long since you used it last?

This is all for now. Hope to hear from you soon.

[Again in his shorthand:] *I love you, and I will always love you*

> Your Devoted,
> Charles

PS I'm working on my grandson, Bill, to take us somewhere for a date soon. I'll let you know when I am successful.

Feb. 1, 1998

Dearest Rosemarie,

I so enjoyed your last letter. It's been over two weeks since I last saw you. Time is really flying, and I hope it does not pass us by!

Any hoo, my grandson, Bill, and his eternal girlfriend, Cathy, plan to come down on Saturday, the 7th, to take me to a family birthday party in Merchantville. That's up your way. We're all staying overnight at my niece Mary's house, and they'll take me home on Sunday. Bill says we can stop to see you on our way back, so I'm wondering if you will be free? I surely do hope so. We'll discuss it on Wednesday when I call. Au revoir. Till we meet again, Sweetheart.

> Your Devoted,
> Charles

Chapter 48

The morning after the birthday party, Charles, Bill, Cathy, and the rest of the family sat at the dining-room table catching up on family news long after breakfast. Finally, at ten thirty, Charles stood up, thanked Mary for her hospitality, and said, "We've got to get going, Mary. I have a stop to make before we go home. Are there any flower shops around here that are open on Sundays?"

Mary told him about a shop in the next town and explained how to get there. With that, everyone else got up from the table and began to clear the dishes. Bill took Charles aside. "Pop Pop, if you want to have a good visit with Rosemarie, we should go right now. Look out the window. It's pouring rain. If we stop at a flower shop, that will cut your visit short with Rosemarie. Cathy and I would like to be on the road home before one."

"Oh, this rain won't last long," Charles said. "Last night the weatherman said it's supposed to slack off close to noon. I've been thinking, if you take me to get the flowers, it will be almost twelve o'clock by the time we get to Rosemarie's. How 'bout I treat the four of us to lunch? There's a cozy tavern just a couple of blocks from her place. I think you and Cathy would like it. What do you say? We'll want to eat before we head for home anyway. Won't we?"

"Yeah, I guess so."

"OK, Pop Pop, you win." Bill laughed. He knew it was useless to argue when Pop Pop set his mind on something.

They said their good-byes to Mary and her family and headed to the Clover Flower Shoppe. It was raining so hard when they got there that Cathy had second thoughts about Charles going inside.

"Pop Pop, you have your good suit on. Why don't you tell me what you want and I'll go in and get it?"

"No, thanks. I'm not sure what I want. I have to see it. Just give me the umbrella. I'll be all right."

Agitated, Bill stepped into the conversation. "We'll help you, Pop Pop, if you insist on going in. He hopped out of the car, opened the doors for Charles and Cathy, and the three of them proceeded into the shop. Cathy held the umbrella over Charles. Bill held firmly onto his grandfather's arm. All of them were getting wet.

Charles took his time looking at everything before deciding on a dozen pink roses. Bill kept his irritation to himself. He knew this was important to his grandfather. Finally, after twenty minutes, they were all back in the car and on their way.

The rain stopped by the time they reached Rosemarie's house, just as Charles predicted. "You two might as well stay in the car," he said as he opened the car door. I'll go in with the flowers and tell Rosemarie we're going out to lunch. She'll be happy about that."

"Pop Pop, let me at least help you to the door with the flowers," said Bill. "That's quite an armful."

"I'll be all right, Bill. Stay put."

Bill and Cathy watched nervously as Charles shuffled up the sidewalk, flowers in hand, to the steps at the front door. He grasped the wrought-iron rail with his free hand and climbed slowly up the four steps. Before he reached the landing, the door opened. There stood Rosemarie.

"Charles, I'm so glad you're here," she said. A smile of relief spread across her face. "I was beginning to worry with all the rain we've had. Come on in."

"Sorry we're late," Charles said as he stepped through the doorway. "But I have a good excuse. These are for you, my dear," he said, placing the roses in her arms.

Before she could say a word, Charles closed the door behind him.

"Wow! I wonder what she thought of the roses," Cathy said as she watched the scene from the car window.

Bill laughed and said, "I'm wondering what's going on behind the closed door. My pop pop is something else."

"Your pop pop is so romantic," Cathy mused. "You should take a page out of his book!"

Ten minutes later, Charles and Rosemarie emerged from the house, faces aglow. Arm in arm, they descended the steps. When they reached the car, Bill jumped out to open the door. "Hi, Rosemarie. Nice to meet you."

"Nice to see you in person, too, Bill. I understand we're going out to lunch."

"That's Pop Pop's idea. Looks like we're going on a double date. I'd like you to meet my girlfriend, Cathy."

Chapter 49

The Red Brick Tavern was only two blocks from Rosemarie's home. Bill had to admit it was not an inconvenience. In fact, he rather liked it when they got inside. It was cozy and dark—even in the daytime—and both he and Cathy were pleased with the music. Surprisingly, it was rock and roll—their kind of music—but toned down a bit for the lunch crowd.

Curious, Bill asked as they waited to be seated, "How did you know about this place, Pop Pop?"

"I passed it on my way to Rosemarie's in July and made a mental note it might be a nice place for a date sometime." Charles laughed. "And here we are."

The hostess came over to them and asked if they wanted a table or a booth.

Charles spoke up immediately. "We'd like a booth, in the corner, please."

Rosemarie smiled.

As soon as they were seated, Charles announced, "Order whatever you want from the menu, everybody. Don't look at the price. It's my treat. And order a drink, too, if you like, but nothing too strong for you, Bill—you have to drive."

Bill grinned. "I was thinking about a beer."

"Good choice." Winking at Rosemarie, Charles said, "How about a Manhattan, Rosemarie? We don't get many opportunities like this."

"That sounds good."

Bill's eyebrows shot up. Cathy's eyes opened wide.

Once the drinks were served, the two couples relaxed, chatted back and forth, and enjoyed the spontaneous party. When they finished their meal, Charles said, "Bill, why don't you take Cathy for a walk before our long ride home? There are lots of shops around here. She would probably like to check them out."

"But, Pop Pop..." Bill started to say something, but the look in his grandfather's eyes stopped him cold.

Taking Cathy's hand he stood up and said, "OK. We'll be back in an hour."

When they were gone, Charles put his arm around Rosemarie, gave her a kiss, and said, "Well, this wasn't exactly what I wanted for our next date, but it will do for now."

"It was wonderful. I enjoyed the lunch tremendously—especially since I wasn't expecting it. The crab cake platter was delicious. Bill and Cathy are such good company, too. They don't seem to mind being with us at all."

"They're good kids. They've been dating a long time. He usually brings her along when he comes to see me. Her grandparents have been gone for a while, and she's kind of adopted me. We get along fine. I wish Bill would get his act together and ask her to marry him. Enough about them. Let's talk about us.

"I'm feeling much better now that I'm back home again. I've been trying to think of other things we can do together. Today was a little experiment, and it seemed to work well. So maybe I can set up some more double dates with Bill and Cathy."

"That would be fun, but I hate to take advantage of them. I'm sure there are other things they would rather do than be with two old people."

"Well, we'll see. Things come up—just like the birthday party. Something else might turn up. We just have to be ready to move if the opportunity presents itself."

Chapter 50

Still basking in the memory of their date the day before, Charles began to focus on his valentine for Rosemarie the next morning. He had an idea for something special, but Valentine's Day was only a week away, so he had no time to waste. After breakfast, he put his dishes in the sink, wiped the table clean, and placed a call to Dave Jackson, his next-door neighbor. He asked if he could borrow his tape recorder for a special project.

Charles often taped old songs for his friends and neighbors, so Dave was glad to lend the machine. He dropped it off a few minutes later on his way to the store. Charles immediately took it to the den and placed it on an old, beat-up card table near the window beside his own tape recorder and an ancient RCA record player. From shelves that lined the walls, he pulled record after record, carefully sorting them into a specific order before placing them on the spindle. Satisfied that all the preliminary work was done, he drove to a drugstore two blocks away for the items he needed to complete his masterpiece.

By one o'clock he was home again with his supplies. He grabbed a quick bite to eat and headed to the den to continue his project. Suddenly, he felt very tired. He put the bag from the drugstore down beside his La-Z-Boy chair and decided to rest for a few minutes. Closing his eyes, he relaxed and left reality.

He was standing along the dance floor at their graduation party at Palmer. Rosemarie, so lovely in her pink taffeta dress, danced by. She looked at him with her big, brown eyes and smiled. Boldly, he tapped her partner on the shoulder and asked Rosemarie to dance. She nodded. He took her in his arms. Beautiful Rosemarie—all his—eyes sparkling and dark, wavy hair scented with roses. They danced and danced the night away—her body next to his...

An hour passed and Charles woke up trembling. All smiles, he recalled the remnants of his dream and wished that it really had happened that way.

Shaking sleep from his mind, he reached for the white plastic bag beside his chair and carried it to his desk where he emptied the contents. Selecting batteries and a recording tape, he replaced the batteries in both tape players and put a new tape in his. He took a small microphone from the top drawer of his desk and placed it in front of his record player and turned it on. Quickly, he flicked the ON button on his tape recorder and sat down to listen. Sounds flowed from one machine to the other. After a few minutes of music, Charles spoke briefly into the microphone and then sang along with an old-time crooner, inserting personal remarks as he went along.

He continued this process with other songs and stories until that tape was full. He did the same with the second tape; only he stopped both the recorder and the record player before the end. Pulling a tape he recorded on the beach years ago from a box on the floor, he placed that in Dave's machine near the microphone. As he turned the two recorders on, Charles closed his eyes and tried to imagine Rosemarie's reaction to his finale.

Chapter 51

Rosemarie wondered, as she walked home from church on February 14, if Charles would send her a card. She hadn't received a valentine since Mike passed away, but Charles might send one. He was always so thoughtful. Earlier in the week, she had mailed him some homemade heart-shaped cookies, with a little note telling him how much she had enjoyed their double date with Bill and his girlfriend. She loved surprises like that, and the pink roses he brought were still so beautiful on her dining-room table.

On the way to bowling later that morning, Carol, her driver, asked, "What do you think Charles will give you for Valentine's Day, Rosemarie?"

She laughed. "Oh, I doubt I'll get anything. We're just friends."

"Come on now. Remember he's your mysterious Romeo. He'll do something."

Later at the alley, when the team sat down to put on their shoes, Mary Finch speculated, "I bet he'll send you chocolates in a heart-shaped box."

Blood rushed to her face as she said, "Oh, get out of here. We aren't kids, you know. Maybe I'll get a card."

"Romeo will do better than that, as romantic as he is," another teammate commented. "My guess is he'll give you a diamond."

Rosemarie laughed. "He doesn't have any way of getting up here, so I know he's not going to do that."

"He's surprised you before."

Their teasing made Rosemarie curious. She couldn't wait to get a look at the mail.

When she returned home at noon, her mailbox was full. Quickly she scanned each envelope for Charles's handwriting. Nothing from Charles! Her hopeful smile disappeared. She was expecting at least a card.

She kept busy. Her ironing basket was empty, so she ironed some sheets. Her house was clean, but she vacuumed anyway.

No card, no chocolates, no phone call. Her spirits were at rock bottom by late afternoon.

Then the doorbell rang. A deliveryman in a dark-brown uniform stood on her front step, with a fat, brown envelope in hand.

"Special delivery for Rosemarie Mulholland," he announced the minute she opened the door.

"That's me."

The man thrust the package toward her and said, "Sign here, please."

Rosemarie's heart skipped a beat. The package was from Charles!

When the driver left, she closed the door and immediately sat down on the love seat. With shaky hands, she tore open the bulky envelope. Inside she found a large pink envelope and two small packages wrapped in pink paper. One package had #1 printed on the outside with the words "Play this one first". The other package read simply #2. She put the small packages on the tea table in front of her and opened the pink envelope first. The card inside had two beautiful pink roses on the front, cascading from the top to the lower left-hand side. The greeting began on the right in striking rose-colored foil letters.

Why do I love you so much?
Because
you're a part of my favorite memories
as well as my most important dreams.
Why
do I love you so much?

Because
I can't imagine what life would be like without love,
and I can't imagine what love
would be like without you.

Inside:

My Darling Rosemarie:
Happy Valentine's Day
February 14th
and
Every Day

All My LOVE
Charles

Rosemarie smiled at Charles's drawing at the bottom of the card. It was so like him to add his own romantic touch.

The two small packages intrigued her.

Brows knit tightly, she tore the paper off package number one and stared. A cassette tape with a hand-printed label, "When You and I Were Seventeen," lay in her lap. She couldn't imagine what this was all about. Quickly she opened the other package, and finding another tape, she took them both to the stereo at the other end of the room.

Puzzled, she stood in front of the machine, trying to figure out what to do. She used the radio in the stereo all the time, but Mike was the only one who knew how to use the tape machine. She had never paid attention to what he did. Now she was stymied. She wanted to hear these tapes. Sorting through booklets in a folder in the stereo cabinet, she finally found the directions she needed. Twenty frustrating minutes later, Charles's voice filled the room. Captivated, Rosemarie dropped to a comfortable chair and listened intently as he sang in a shaky voice:

"When you and I were seventeen,

And all the world was new..."

When the song ended, Charles said:

"Now listen, Rosemarie, as I tell you the story of two teenagers, a girl and a boy, over seventy years ago. That's right—seventy years. It is now 1998, but it was in the spring of 1926 that these two young people started school at Palmer Business School in central Philadelphia..."

The tape continued for forty-five minutes. Charles talked directly to Rosemarie at times; other times he sang or hummed along with Bing Crosby or others like him as they crooned romantic songs from the twenties, thirties and forties. He told of their days at Palmer and how he became enamored with her. At the end he said, "I always regretted that I didn't speak to you back then, Rosemarie."

When the tape stopped, Rosemarie's face was rosy; a smile danced across it. Delighted with her one-of-a-kind valentine, she removed tape number one, replaced it with tape number two, entitled "Girl of My Dreams," and turned the machine back on. Charles, accompanied by an orchestra, sang.

"Girl of my Dreams I love you,

Honest I do,

You are so sweet,

If I could just hold your charm once in my arms,

Then life would be complete...

After all's said and done, there's only one.

Girl of my dreams,

Rosemarie, it's you."

Charles continued talking and singing to Rosemarie for another half hour. Then, without warning, the tape stopped, and there was silence. Gradually, the sounds of waves crashing, seagulls squawking, and a boat whistling off in the distance filled the room. Mesmerized, Rosemarie listened as soothing music joined the beach sounds, and Charles spoke:

"Although my home is two blocks from the Delaware Bay, Rosemarie, sometimes when the wind is right, I hear the waves crashing on the shore. Can you hear them? When there's a storm, I hear the ferry whistles, too. Must be rough out there now."

Charles was silent for the next four minutes as sounds of the bay filtered through gentle music. Then he spoke again:

"Storm seems to have subsided now." Birdsong replaced the beach sounds against the background music.

Then Charles said, "Sun's going down—getting dark." Five more minutes of soft romantic music. Then Charles sang along with Dick Haymes: "So take my heart in sweet surrender, and tenderly say that I'm the one you love and care for till the end of time." The music stopped, and Charles said, "I love you, Rosemarie. I always will, I really will, till the end of time. Happy Valentine's Day, sweetheart."

The tape stopped. Rosemarie sat staring off into space. Tears streamed down her face, unnoticed, onto her new red-knit top. In the silence, she thought back over the past five years. This fling with Charles had been such fun. She had enjoyed the mystique when he entered her life, been thrilled with the experience of dating again in her eighties, and was flattered by Charles's romantic dates, kisses, and long phone calls. He totally ignored their age and acted like a boyfriend many decades younger. She liked that, but after this very special gift, she realized that their relationship was not a fling for Charles. He really cared about her, really loved her. Were her feelings changing, too?

Chapter 52

Charles called at six thirty that evening, unable to wait one more minute to hear Rosemarie's reaction to his valentine. He was not disappointed. He barely said, "Happy Valentine's Day, dear," when she started.

"Charles, your gift was wonderful! I loved your beautiful card. And I still can't believe you made those tapes! What a clever idea—and so romantic. How did you do it? It was all so wonderful it made me cry." Rosemarie sniffled. "I'm still crying. I feel like I'm Queen for a Day!"

"Well, you are my queen, but I didn't expect you to cry, for goodness' sake!" Charles laughed. "I just wanted to make you happy."

"Oh, you did. You did!"

"Well, I was happy with your surprise, too!" Charles said. "Thanks for the nice note, and those chocolate-covered heart cookies were delicious. I figured you must have made them. I can't imagine you buying them in a bakery."

"No, they didn't come from a bakery. I made them just for you."

"Well, I guess we're not too old for Valentine's Day, are we? I just wish we could be together more often—especially today—so I could show you how much you mean to me. I talked with Bill last week, and we have a couple of double dates lined up, but what I really want is to be with you every day. What do you think about that, Rosemarie?"

Caught off guard, she sighed and said, "I don't know, Charles. I do care about you a lot, but it's complicated at our age. I have to think about it."

"I'm not going to pressure you, but please think about it. If you agree, we'll work out the problems somehow. I have an idea."

Chapter 53

Rosemarie shared bits and pieces of her Valentine's Day with friends and family. She described the card but not his message. She gave lavish details about the tapes but not a word about her conversation with Charles.

Her daughters and lady friends from church, the bowling alley, and the beauty shop were delighted to hear the latest edition of her love story. They all agreed that Rosemarie's Romeo was a winner in the romance department. None of them had ever received a valentine as unique as hers.

Rosemarie enjoyed being in the limelight, but she dared not tell any of the girls about Charles's proposal. She had been in a quandary ever since he mentioned it. What should she do? Charles was not considering their age at all. He had definitely invaded her heart and had long since left the status of Phantom Romeo, but still she wasn't sure how far she was willing to go to keep him in her life. If she married him, where they would live? He couldn't manage the stairs in her house, and she wasn't sure if she wanted to move to Cape May—so far from her church and her friends. Finally, although they never discussed it, they were nearing ninety. How much longer could they care for their homes and themselves?

Charles didn't waste one minute worrying about the future or their relationship. He planned two double dates for them with Bill and Cathy—one at the Red Brick Tavern for lunch in March and the other at a dinner theater in Moorestown in April. They always had a good time.

The young couple treated them more like friends than grandparents, and that made everyone more comfortable. Charles made certain on each occasion that he and Rosemarie had some private time together, but he refrained from mentioning his proposal again as he had promised. Rosemarie would come around—he was convinced of that. But nothing was easy.

One day, in May, Rosemarie received a call from Bill.

"Rosemarie, Pop Pop had a fall this morning and is in the hospital again. I thought you would want to know."

"Oh, Bill, I'm so sorry. Did he hurt himself?"

"He'll be OK. He sprained his ankle when he went out to get the paper and has to be off of it for a while. They are keeping him in the hospital overnight to make sure he didn't have a mini stroke. My dad is down here trying to convince him to come live with him and my mom until he heals, but he is not going for it."

"I wish I could help, Bill. Is there anything I can do?"

"I'm sure he would appreciate a call from you. He's in the same hospital as before, but he has a phone in his room this time. He's in room 206."

"Thanks for letting me know. I'll call him this afternoon."

Before contacting Charles, Rosemarie called Anne at work. Her voice sounded worried and strained as she told her about Bill's call.

"I can't take you down today, Mother, or even tomorrow," Anne said. "One of the girls is out sick this week, and we are so busy. Charles knows your situation. He'll understand. Call him."

"I intend to call him. Bill said he has a phone in his room, but I feel I should do more. He's been so good to me. His son wants him to stay with him in Quakertown until he heals, but Bill said he won't do it. They still don't know why he fell. The doctors are checking to see if he had a stroke. I'm so worried. I'd like to take care of him when he goes home."

"Whoa—wait a minute, Mother!" Anne said. "Let's talk about this. He has a family who cares about him. They'll figure this out. What if he fell again? You couldn't get him up. It would complicate things if the family had to worry about you, too."

"I guess you're right, but I feel so helpless," Rosemarie said. "I don't know what to do."

"Call him. Have a long chat. That will cheer him up. He was lucky not to break any bones. Don't make a big deal out of this. He'll be OK."

Rosemarie knew Anne was right. Charles was lucky the fall wasn't worse, but still she couldn't keep from worrying about him. She realized now more than ever how much Charles meant to her.

"All right, I'll call him for now," she said. "I'll talk to you later."

Rosemarie called the hospital immediately and asked for Charles. The phone rang and rang. At last a strange male voice answered, "Hello."

Rosemarie's body tensed.

"Charles, is that you?"

"No, this is John. I'm in the next bed. Hold on, I'll hand the phone to Charles."

Charles, sounding cheerful, finally answered, "Hello."

"Charles, this is Rosemarie. How are you?"

"I'm OK, dear. Don't worry, it's just a sprain. It only hurts when I walk. Ha-ha. It's so good to hear your voice."

"Bill said his dad wants to take you back to Quakertown with him for a while."

"Well, I'm not doing that! They've been trying to convince me to move in with them ever since I had that heart problem last fall. The whole family thinks I shouldn't be living alone anymore."

"Well, what are you going to do? You are going to need help. I wish I could come down to help you."

"I do, too. It probably wouldn't be a good idea right now, though. The next time we visit, how about if we discuss our being together again? You said you had to think about it. Remember?"

"I remember," Rosemarie said quietly.

"Besides," Charles continued, "Bill talked to someone here, and they are getting me a home-health aide for a few hours a day to cook and help me out when I go home, which I hope is tomorrow. I'll use a walker to get around until I can put weight on my foot again. Don't worry, I'll be back in shape in no time. I'm working on Bill for another date when my foot is healed."

"I hope you get better soon. I enjoy our dates so much."

"I'll do my best, sweetheart. I'll call you from home tomorrow. Love you."

For the first time, Rosemarie, in a barely audible voice, replied, "Love you, too."

Beaming, Charles handed the phone back to John.

John looked at him in awe and said, "Wow, buddy, sorry I couldn't help but hear. I'm jealous. Sounds like you have a girlfriend on the hook. She must be someone special."

"Oh, she's special all right. I'm trying to get her to marry me."

John didn't comment, but looking at the old man in the bed beside him, he thought, *Lots of luck, buddy.*

He didn't know Charles.

Chapter 54

After Charles left the hospital, the phone dates between him and Rosemarie increased from one day a week to every day. Things were happening so fast they both felt the need to keep in touch often. Rosemarie came down with shingles and spent six weeks in misery. The calls of concern from Charles comforted her—kept her spirits up and made her yearn for him by her side.

Charles had his own issues. His children were pressuring him to move to a retirement community closer to them. They took turns taking him to these places, but Charles told Rosemarie in his daily calls, "I'm not going anywhere without you."

With all this going on, Rosemarie was unsettled. At night, after her busy daytime activities—after Charles's phone call ended—she would spend long sleepless hours thinking about his proposal, thinking how impractical it was at this time of their lives to get married, and wondering if he moved in with his family in Pennsylvania or Texas if she would ever see him again.

Charles, in the meantime, was losing no sleep. He was making plans. His children meant well, but they did not understand his deep feelings for Rosemarie. Although they were aware of his relationship with her, it never occurred to them that she would have to be considered in any plan for his future. So, unknown to his children, Charles involved the only person who would understand and help. Bill would be on his side with anything regarding Rosemarie. Charles was certain of that.

The next Saturday he asked Bill to drive him to a small town not far from Rosemarie's home. Charles did what he wanted to do there. The following Wednesday a postcard arrived for Rosemarie, with his plan for them spelled out.

The card showed three impressive Victorian-style buildings. Each had a wide wraparound porch furnished with white, wicker furniture. The landscape surrounding the buildings was breathtaking—green, spacious lawns, with colorful beds of spring flowers and a winding drive-way from the street lined with pink and white dogwoods.

Across the bottom of the postcard were the following four words in bold, white script:

Victorian Gardens Retirement Community

Rosemarie was dumbfounded. Turning the card over, she read:

Dearest Rosemarie,
I have applied for residence here. It's a very nice place especially because it is close to you. Perhaps you would like to live here too-with me. Think about it, sweetheart. and will till the end of time!

Charles

Chapter 55

The prospect of leaving her beloved home and moving into a retirement community with Charles stunned her at first, even though he had hinted at it before. It made Rosemarie face the fact that she could not delay her decision much longer. Age ninety was looming on the horizon. Arthritis was making it difficult for her to do the things she enjoyed. She could no longer care for her home the way she always did, and she knew that this was her last year to bowl. Her daughters offered to have her move in with them, but her heart was telling her otherwise. Charles was pressuring her, in a gentle way, to spend the rest of his days with him. Should she stop fretting and live in the moment? She prayed for an answer.

Charles spoke only once about the postcard, wanting to know how she felt about the place and his message.

"It's a lovely place, Charles. I am thinking about what you are asking and will give you my answer soon."

"OK, sweetheart, but don't wait too long. In the meantime, I've got some news for you."

"What?"

"I called Bill last night to see if he could take us on another date now that we are both off the sick list, and guess what?"

"I can't imagine."

"He finally popped the question to Cathy. They are going to be married in September."

"Oh, I'm so happy for them, Charles. They are such a nice couple, and they have been so good to us."

"Yeah, it's great for them but not so good for us. We can no longer count on them for dates. Bill said they need every weekend to get things together for the wedding. Any chance Anne could take us somewhere soon?"

"I'm not sure. Her weekends are usually very busy. It might be a while, but I'll call her tonight and see what I can do."

"Good. Be sure you let her know that we'll need some time alone. After all, I haven't seen you for almost four months. We have some important things to hash over."

Chapter 56

Rosemarie wasted no time in placing the call. It was four o'clock. Anne was still at work, but she called anyway.

"Are you busy?" she asked when Anne answered her phone.

"Not at the moment. Is anything wrong?"

"Nothing's wrong. I just have a favor to ask you."

"What is it?"

"Well, I haven't seen Charles for almost four months, and I was wondering—now that we are both feeling better—if you could spare a day to take me to Cape May for a visit. Charles said he would treat to lunch if you can swing it."

"My weekends are packed for the next month," Anne replied. "Can we talk about this tonight?" Hearing a deep sigh from the other end of the line, she added quickly, "Well, maybe I can take a vacation day during the week. Another call is coming in now. Mother, I'll have to call you back later. I'll speak to my boss before I leave today and call you tonight, OK?"

"OK. Thanks."

Rosemarie was sitting at her desk in front of the phone when it rang at seven o'clock.

"Anne?"

"Yes, it's me. I have next Friday off—the fifteenth."

"Oh, that's wonderful! Thank you so much."

"Did you and Charles discuss where you want to go?"

"Not yet. We were waiting to see if you could get a day off first."

"Well, I have a suggestion, if you and Charles approve."

"Anywhere is OK with us as long as we can have some time alone."

"How about a round-trip ferry ride from Cape May to Delaware?" Anne asked. "It would take most of the day. They have a nice restaurant on board, and you'd have plenty of time to visit with Charles."

"That would be great! Charles will love it. He lives right near the ferry."

"I know. That's what made me think of it. And guess what? Remember my old friend, Judy Carter?"

"Sure. She was your best friend in high school."

"Well, she's back home visiting her family for a few weeks. She called me to see if we could get together while she's here. I told her about the ferry trip and asked if she would like to be my date for the day. She was delighted and can't wait to see you and your boyfriend. So that's the plan. Make sure Charles is OK with it, and I'll make the final arrangements."

"I know he will be all for it. Go ahead with the arrangements. I've never been on the ferry before. This should be fun."

Minutes later she was on the phone with Charles.

He listened to the plans and said immediately, "That's a great idea! When are we going?"

"Next Friday, the fifteenth. Is that OK with you?"

"Perfect! We can spend the whole day together this time. Anne and her friend won't want to hang around with us old folks. The ferry is huge. They can find plenty to do."

Charles could not believe his good fortune. This was exactly what he had been waiting for—a golden opportunity to spend time alone with Rosemarie. He knew everything about the ferry and had the latest schedule. His head swirled with plans for their date. In the days that followed, it was he who determined their departure time and he who meticulously formulated a scheme to ensure their privacy.

Chapter 57

*D*ate day dawned sunny, cloudless, and gorgeous. It was a day that made you glad to be alive. Rosemarie was in high spirits on the way to Cape May.

It was clear to Anne from the moment she pulled up in front of his house that Charles intended to make the most of every minute. Before she could even get out of the car to help, he had maneuvered himself down his front steps to the sidewalk, then to the car, without his cane.

He was dressed to impress in sharply creased, white summer slacks; a light-blue shirt that complimented his blue eyes; and white casual shoes. Looking very snazzy for a man his age, he climbed into the backseat with Rosemarie, greeted Anne and Judy, and began to give directions to the ferry without further ado.

It was Anne's plan that they all stay on the ferry for a round trip. She told Rosemarie on the way down that most of the travelers would get off in Delaware to shop the outlets or to visit the charming town of Lewes. But because this would involve a lot of walking, she thought it would be easier on Charles and Rosemarie if they all stayed on the ferry, had lunch, and enjoyed the afternoon on the bay.

When they reached the ferry parking lot, Anne and Judy began gathering sunglasses, sweaters, and handbags, but apparently not fast enough for Charles. Before they knew it, he had hustled Rosemarie out of the backseat and into the crowd surging toward the ferry. They were nowhere in sight by the time Anne and Judy reached the ticket booth.

The girls had no choice but to buy the round-trip tickets that had been discussed with Rosemarie and get on the ferry.

"I can't believe they got away from us," Anne said.

Judy laughed. "I think it's a riot! Looks like they're anxious to be alone."

"You're probably right. That's OK. After all, that's why we're here in the first place."

They wandered the ferry randomly, looking for the elusive couple, but not trying too hard. Eventually, they spotted them in the cocktail lounge at the front of the boat. They were sitting at the bar, each with a glass of wine in hand at ten thirty in the morning.

Charles had his arm around Rosemarie's shoulders, and they were so deeply engrossed in conversation that Anne and Judy chose not to intrude. Instead, they found comfortable seats in the sun on the upper deck. When the boat docked, they stayed there as other passengers hurried to the exit. After the travelers from Delaware came aboard and the ferry left the dock, Anne said, "I'm ready for lunch. How about you, Judy?"

"Me too. I'm starved!"

They headed across the deck to the stairway that led to the restaurant on the lower level. On the second step, Anne happened to glance back at the dock, and that's when she saw them—a balding man in white pants and a blue shirt and a petite lady in a pink, flowered dress walking hand in hand with the crowd headed for the trolley to Lewes. It was all she could do to get down the remaining steps safely. The scene was hysterical.

The aged Romeo and Juliet, happy as birds flying the coop, and the two chaperones stuck on the ferry headed in the opposite direction. Anne and Judy didn't laugh. They were responsible for this couple, weren't they? What could they do? They opted for a drink in the lounge and had just placed their order when the loudspeakers overhead blared the captain's "Welcome Aboard" announcement, followed by a request for Anne Maloney to report immediately to the information booth on the main deck.

"Go ahead. I'll wait here," Judy said.

Anne jumped up, alarmed, mumbling, "What now?"

Nerves frazzled, she rushed to the main deck.

"I'm Anne Maloney," she said breathlessly to the man at the booth. Her legs felt like Jell-O as he reached under the counter.

"Hi, Anne."

Handing her a white envelope with her name on it, he said, "An elderly gentleman gave me this right before we docked in Delaware. He said it was real important that I give it to you after we were underway returning to Cape May. Hope everything is OK."

"Me too," she said. "Thanks."

Leaving the booth, Anne tore open the envelope and found a note inside, wrapped around a small envelope, with a blue crab in the corner.

Dear Anne,

Sorry we did not follow your plan for today. This gift certificate is our way of thanking you for the wonderful chance you gave us to be together. Enjoy your meal with Judy at "The Blue Crab Cafe." It's a nice restaurant on the Boardwalk in Cape May. We will meet you at the fudge shop on the Boardwalk at 8:30. Please don't worry about us. We want to make the most of this day. Thanks again,

Charles

Chapter 58

"What a fantastic day!" Charles said enthusiastically as he and Rosemarie walked slowly toward the trolley. He squeezed her hand and said, "I have big plans for the two of us."

Rosemarie frowned. Glancing back at the ferry and then at him, she said, "Charles, do you think we did the right thing just taking off like this? I've never done anything like this in my life. What will the girls think?"

"Ha! Remember, this day was Anne's idea. They'll be fine," he said as he guided her onto the trolley. "Besides, I left them a note."

"You did? You think of everything!" she said, her face now wreathed in smiles.

When the trolley stopped in Lewes at twelve thirty, Charles led Rosemarie away from the crowd and down a red-brick alley until they came upon a small two-story building facing the waterfront. Rounding the faded, blue clapboard structure, the couple climbed three wooden steps to the deck of the Bayside Cafe. As they paused on the top step to look over the waterfront, Charles glanced at Rosemarie. He was pleased to see her eyes widen with pleasure.

"This is the first stop on our way to OZ," Charles joked, but Rosemarie didn't hear a word. She was too enthralled with the scene—marshmallow clouds drifting in the bright-blue sky, boats of all sizes bobbing on the bay, seagulls soaring overhead, and the bay kissed by the midday sun glistening like glass. It was all so perfect. Rosemarie took deep breaths, inhaling the fresh air.

Her worries about the future vanished with the wind, and a feeling of freedom and contentment came over her.

"This is wonderful, Charles," she said. "Thank you so much for bringing me here. I feel so good!"

"Me, too. How about we get something to eat?" he said, eyeing the bay window on the second floor of the cafe.

"OK, I am beginning to feel hungry."

A smiling, suntanned waitress with a ponytail met them inside the door.

"Where would you folks like to sit?" she asked sweetly, noticing with amusement that the old man and woman were holding hands.

"Upstairs in the window," Charles replied without hesitation.

"OK. I'm Carol, your waitress. Follow me." She grabbed two menus and led the way. "Be careful on the steps," she warned, wondering why two old people would want to climb upstairs when there was plenty of seating on the first floor.

"We'll be OK," Charles replied, guiding Rosemarie toward the stairs. He had been here before. He knew Rosemarie would love the second floor and that she would agree it was worth climbing the ten steps. Entering the dark, cozy room, Rosemarie and Charles stopped to catch their breath. Their waitress—unaware that her elderly customers were lagging behind—forged ahead. At the window, when she stopped and turned to speak to them, she realized they were still standing at the top of the stairs. Quickly, she retraced her steps and asked, "Are you two OK?"

"Sure," Charles answered, offering a plausible excuse for their delay. "We were just admiring the decor."

"This nautical atmosphere is terrific. I almost feel like I'm on a ship!" Rosemarie gushed.

Small, metal lanterns—centered on blue and white checked tablecloths—flickered brightly in the dimly lit room, casting shadows across a long mural on the wall facing them.

"That scene looks so real I can almost hear the captain shouting to his shipmates during the storm," Charles remarked.

"I love those little lanterns on the tables," Rosemarie said. "They look exactly like the lanterns on the deck of the ship in the painting."

"As a matter of fact, they are replicas," Carol remarked. "The owner of the cafe has a friend—a tin craftsman—who made them for her. I love them, too."

Charles interrupted, "Hey, ladies, I'm starved!"

Carol laughed. "OK, I take it you are ready to go to your table now."

"We'll be right behind you this time," Charles answered.

Blue, cotton tieback curtains framed the bay window at Charles's chosen location. As they were seated, sunlight streamed through the panes of glass, illuminating Rosemarie's happy face. Charles grinned as she raved again about the spectacular view. He knew he had chosen wisely.

Carol handed the couple their menus, announced the specials of the day, and waited for their orders. She was fascinated with them and happy to be their waitress. As the pair decided on their meal, she could see that they were in no hurry. She eyed the rest of the room. Two other couples were finishing their meals at tables near the mural. She made a mental note to steer any new customers to seating downstairs.

When she came back with their crab cake sandwiches twenty minutes later, she was amused to see that the old couple had moved their chairs close together, facing the window. The gentleman had his arm around the little lady, and Carol was sure he gave her a kiss. Both were startled when she came up behind them to deliver their meals.

"You don't mind if we rearrange your furniture a bit, do you?" Charles asked with a twinkle in his eye.

Carol smiled. "I don't care at all. You two are up here all by yourselves now. You can get nice and cozy."

Charles laughed. Rosemarie giggled.

After Carol left, they ate in silence. When they were finished, Charles turned to face Rosemarie. He took her hand in his as he spoke. "We've talked about everything, Rosemarie—the beautiful day, the ferry, Anne and Judy, and this restaurant. Now let's talk about us. You know how I feel about you—the same way I felt when I first saw you over seventy years ago. You didn't know me then, but I believe you know me pretty well now. You haven't given me an answer about moving to Victorian Gardens. What do you think? It's a beautiful place. I'm sure you would like it. Think how nice it would be for us to be in the same place and never have to ask anyone else to bring us together. Who knows how much time we have left? Let's make the most of it." Charles stopped talking. "Now it's your turn."

Rosemarie's eyes were moist as she answered, "Charles, I do care for you very much, and we always have such a good time together, but this is a huge step for me. I have been thinking about Victorian Gardens a lot. The girls have asked me to come live with them, too, and I have considered that also. I don't know which way to turn. Our relationship has been like a fairy tale to me. I want it to continue, but..."

"What?" Charles asked.

"I've always been a practical person, and I'm wondering if moving in with you at this time of our lives is wise," Rosemarie replied.

"I'm not asking you to just move in with me, dearest. I'm asking you to marry me and sail off into the sunset with me." Charles pulled her close and kissed her wet cheek.

"Charles, I don't know what to say. Marriage at our age!" Rosemarie giggled. "What would people say?"

"I don't care what anyone says but you. What do *you* say?"

"I've been praying about this and looking for a sign of which way to go."

"OK. That's enough for now. Let's enjoy the day. We'll talk about it later."

An hour passed before Carol returned to their table, but the couple didn't seem to notice. They were too busy talking. She asked if they wanted dessert and wondered what in the world old people had to talk about.

Rosemarie hesitated and then said, "No, thanks."

Charles winked at her and said, "Come on, Rosemarie, you have a great figure. You don't have to worry about calories. Have some chocolate ice cream with me and another cup of coffee."

Carol was tickled to see Rosemarie blush and then give in to dessert.

When Carol picked up their order on the first floor, she told the owner and the downstairs staff all about the lovebirds upstairs. One by one they snuck quietly up to the second floor to take a peek.

The desserts were delivered, but Carol did not return with the couple's bill until it was time for her to go home.

"What time is it?" Charles asked as though he suddenly realized how long they had been there.

"Three thirty," Carol replied.

Charles reached for Rosemarie's hand and said, "We have to go. We don't want to be late for the four o'clock trolley back to the ferry."

They stood up quickly and headed to the stairway hand in hand. Carol cleared their table and followed them to the first floor. The room was empty. The lunch crowd was long gone, and according to a sign near the front door, dinner wouldn't be served until five. Oddly, the lunch staff was still there, lingering near the kitchen.

Rosemarie made a comment to the owner when they reached the register near the front door. "Everyone else is gone. I guess we stayed too long." The owner smiled and said, "No problem. We're happy you had a good time. We'd like you to have something to remember your visit with us." Carol came forward and handed Rosemarie the lantern that was on their table.

Tears rolled down her face as she kissed both women. "Thank you so much." Then she held the gift up for all the staff to see and said, "I love this little lantern. I'll never forget this place. We had such a good time, and the food was delicious. Thank you all so much."

Charles stood by beaming as Carol took the lantern from Rosemarie, placed it in a brown bag, and handed it back. He paid their bill, and they said their good-byes. Arm in arm, Charles and Rosemarie meandered down the red-brick alley back to the trolley stop as the owner and staff of the Bayside Cafe watched from the front window with tears in their eyes.

The Last Chapter

*O*nce they settled in their seats outside on the deck of the ferry, Charles let Rosemarie in on the next step in his plan.

"Are you tired, Rosemarie?"

"No. Not at all. I feel great! How about you?"

"I feel great, too!"

"I wonder what the girls will say when we get back."

"We won't be seeing them for a while," Charles replied.

"Why? What do you mean?"

"I gave them a gift certificate for dinner on the boardwalk. We won't be meeting them until eight thirty. It's all in the note I left them."

"Charles, I can't believe it! Where are we going? We don't have a car."

"We'll take the shuttle into town, and then I have another surprise. Now just put your head on my shoulder and rest a bit. We have an hour and a half before we dock."

At six forty-five, the ferry shuttle stopped at a pink-stucco, five-story hotel right across from the beach and boardwalk in Cape May.

"Is this your surprise?" Rosemarie asked, wide-eyed.

"This is it," Charles replied happily as he guided her up the steps of the Victorian Sandcastle.

He knew she loved all things Victorian.

"This place looks so expensive! This is too much after the wonderful lunch we had in Lewes."

"Don't worry about it, my dear. The best is yet to come." Charles grinned mischievously. He led her inside the hotel to the elevator. When the door opened on the fifth floor, Charles took her arm as they crossed the hall to the Crystal Dining Room. Rosemarie gasped at the sight before her.

"I knew you would like it, sweetheart," he said softly.

Dazzling crystal chandeliers shimmered above intimate tables double draped with white and rose-colored linens. Each table was adorned with a crystal bud vase, featuring a perfect pink rose. Fine white china and ornate silverware graced each place, complemented by rose-colored napkins cascading from long-stemmed crystal glasses. Even the ocean, as seen through a glass wall on the far side of the room, fit into the scheme of things, glittering in the early evening like a sea of diamonds.

Charles spoke quietly to the tuxedoed maître d' just inside the entrance. The man glanced down at his reservation book and said, "Yes, Mr. Benson. We do have you down for dinner for two at seven. A table near the piano, right?"

Charles nodded.

A young waiter—handsomely dressed in a white shirt, black tie, and black slacks—appeared from nowhere and led them to their table. With much aplomb he graciously pulled out a chair for Rosemarie and another for Charles.

"Would you folks like a drink?" he asked pleasantly, expecting the balding old man and his elderly companion to order iced tea.

"We would," answered Charles immediately.

The waiter's face registered surprise when Charles leaned toward his lady friend and asked, "How about champagne, Rosemarie?"

Her reply, "Yes, I'd like that," was not the answer the waiter expected.

Smiling, he said, "OK. I'll be back in a few minutes with your drinks and the menu."

"Charles, this is the loveliest restaurant I've ever been to," Rosemarie whispered when the waiter left. "I can't believe it. You're spoiling me. This whole day has been one surprise after the other."

"I'm glad you're having a good time. I wanted this date to be extra special."

"Oh, it is!"

"Good, now relax and pretend we are both twenty years old," he said as he leaned over and planted a kiss on her neck.

Startled, Rosemarie whispered, "Charles! For heaven's sake! What will people think?"

"Who cares?" he asked with a laugh.

The waiter returned with their drinks and took their orders for dinner. When he left, Charles slid his chair closer to Rosemarie's, and raising his glass, he said, "To the girl in my dreams."

Rosemarie smiled, kissed Charles's cheek, and lifting her own glass, said, "To the man in my life."

As they sipped their champagne, a dark-haired man in a white tuxedo sauntered to the center of the room and without fanfare took his place at a sleek mahogany piano. The music he played was old-fashioned, adding to the romantic ambiance. By the time their meals arrived, Charles and Rosemarie felt decades younger, and the subject of marriage came up again.

A young couple at a table near them had been noticing the elderly couple ever since the champagne was served. They overheard the toasts and saw Rosemarie's kiss. They were fascinated and strained to hear the rest of their conversation, but the music muffled their words. The young woman tried not to stare, but right before dessert, out of the corner of her eye, she saw the old gentleman take the woman's hand and whisper something into her ear. The lady smiled. Tears rolled down her cheeks. Looking into his eyes, slowly she nodded yes.

The nosy woman couldn't help but wonder why the old man immediately stood up and walked over to the piano player. He spoke to the musician, who began to page through sheet after sheet of music. Finally, he settled on one piece.

Charles returned to his table with a Cheshire cat grin on his face. The pianist announced, "I have a request from Mr. Charles Benson for an oldie, 'Till the End of Time.'" As the music began, Charles put his arm around Rosemarie. Looking into her eyes, as if there was not another soul in the room, he sang softly to her...

So take my heart in sweet surrender
My darling, as I say that I'm
The one who will love and care for you, Rosemarie,
Till the end of time.

A Word from the Author

As you recall from my note at the start of this book, my son Jerry said the story of his grandmother and her Romeo is "positively the stuff of fairy tales." Now that you have finished *The Girl in His Dreams*, I'm sure you will agree with him. However, Jerry's original e-mail did not end there. I chose to place the rest of his thoughts here.

When I think of the man, I think of the story I got handed later about him falling for Grandmom as a teenager and remembering a single passing glance she made in his direction. Today people would call his experience a teenage crush—a boy hoping and dreaming about what it would be like as a couple, with a girl who doesn't know he exists. Then roll forward 70 years: their paths cross by some twist of destiny, and he is able to get past his crush, talk to her, and ask her out. That in and of itself would be great fiction. It is absolutely fascinating to me as real events.

I barely met the man once. Without even having spoken ten words to him, I found that I liked him and the many things he represented: The old romantic waiting all those years until he and Grandmom both were available again. The slow way he planted himself in her imagination over the years, as she wondered who he was. Then actually stepping forward once the trail led us to him and becoming a new friend to Grandmom, with the ever-present spark of love in the air.

For him to come forward and seek her with apparent wild abandon, at his age, is incredible. He's a hero to me.

Made in the USA
Charleston, SC
06 November 2016